MW01204865

LIVING WITH INTEREST:

INDIAN SUMMER

by:

Robert D. Hammitt

Dedication

I dedicate this book to my family and friends who continued to encourage me long after I'm sure they lost interest in the story itself. Special thanks to those who helped me develop the storyline: Jim, Kathrine, Carrie, Lisa, Karen and Kyle; to my principal editors: Belinda, Karen, Curt, and Sheila; and to those who gave me the most encouragement: Melinda, Marlin, Kara, Jimmy, Carrie, and especially Kyle.

When I started writing this book, I only had the basic concept of banking a day and the after effects it might cause. As I developed the storyline, much of my personal past worked itself into the plot and characters. I had more fun playfully weaving my friends and family into the story than anything else associated with the book. So for that, I sincerely thank each and every person from my past, present, and future who have influenced my life up to this point, and to those I may not even know yet. I'm confident you will step in at the right moment in time to help complete my story.

Living With Interest: *Indian Summer*
Table of Contents

Prologue

Chapters:

Additional Insights:

Prologue:

The explosion reverberated in Levi's ears, setting his entire jaw in pain. While Levi gathered his senses, having been awakened from a deep sleep, his first thought was of the night he had been injured. He quickly regained his whereabouts, as the small house stopped trembling from the lightning's aftershock. With his ears still ringing, he stumbled through the kitchen door into the January night. The air was crisp and charged with electricity, giving the snow on the ground an odd greenish tint.

Levi immediately looked upward, expecting to see towering clouds continuously lit by more lightning; but the sky was completely clear. The near-full moon, accompanied by a blanket of stars, cast dancing shadows in the snow from the tall trees still swaying from the electrical discharge. As Levi's eyes adjusted to the light, he noticed smoke coming from the hill near the house.

When Levi reached the source of the smoke, he realized the lightning must have struck the ancient pole the old Indian woman

had recently shown him. Strangely, the pole was not on fire, yet it had a glow that resembled a horseshoe being worked by a blacksmith. The red-hot timber had a sheen that indicated this was not the first time it had been struck by lightning.

Footsteps in the snow alarmed Levi, until he saw the old woman approaching from the house. Her first words warned Levi to move away from the pole. When they were at a distance she felt was safe, she began to explain what had just happened.

"Levi, tonight begins a journey that will change your life… and those who come after you. The best way to explain all that you must learn is to show you, and that begins here, with the Life Pole of my ancestors… but first, watch, and see I speak the truth."

She pointed to a tree that was near the Life Pole. No sooner than she did, a huge dead limb that had been damaged by the lightning came crashing down and landed exactly where Levi stood moments before.

Levi turned to the old woman and in a quivering voice asked, "How did you know the limb would break like that? I could have been killed."

"Your injuries were many, but not deadly."

Levi was confused by her comment. He hadn't been injured. As he looked at her expression, he wondered if there were more to her words than he understood.

"Knowledge of the future is also knowledge of the past, if our eyes are open. Levi, there is much I must teach you, and little time. Come to the house… you will see how other future events were shaped by the past."

As the trees resumed a still state in the once again calm night, she led him back to the house. A lantern was lit in the front room, where they sat at a small table along with a third person until the sun rose, engaged in the first lesson of this mysterious and life-changing subject.

#

Intersecting Paths:

When the trees in the city park are in full bloom, their towering trunks and full canopies create an image of one consistent flow, reaching toward the sky. Not until autumn do we see the complexity in the network of branches, each pushing the tree upward. Once the trees grow close, their canopies weave together creating a complex pattern of interaction.

Such are the twists and turns in the journey we take with our friends and family. Our paths converge and diverge as a result of the decisions we each make during our lives, but they all lead us forward.

With perspective, we can learn many lessons; not only how to observe our interconnected lives, but also how to truly live. It isn't really our destination or the particular route we select that matters, it's our interaction with others along the way that adds value. Recognizing and embracing the intersection of our paths, builds and supports the branches of our family tree.

#

I. Between Now and Then

I've had an interesting life; although when I was young, I didn't have the perspective to appreciate it.

Today is the day I've been looking forward to for sixteen years. Actually, I've been waiting for this day most of my life, and I'm an old man; but I'll explain how and when I got here in due time.

Time: some say God sees time all at once, everything past, present, and future; all simultaneously. If that's true, our destiny has already been written. However, predestination seems a bit rigid to me. I like to think our free will can influence future events by the decisions we make today. We may or may not ultimately arrive at the same destination, but the branches in our paths can definitely alter how we enjoy our journey. Either way, we only have one day to live at a time, no matter how it may fit into the grand sequence of events. It took observing several generations for me to arrive at this point, and strangely, my story starts and ends at the same place and time - here and now.

Today is my granddaughter Kristine's sixteenth birthday. I'm still getting used to calling her Kristine; she has always been

Kristy to me. Last week, she informed the family that she is too old to be called Kristy. After all, she was about to turn sixteen, she is growing up. My name is Bobby Greenfield, and I can empathize with Kristy as my name has also transitioned. When I started my career, I briefly thought I needed to sound more mature, so I tried "Robert" for a while, but that wasn't me. I quickly decided I preferred a younger, less serious sounding name; so full-circle, I returned to "Bobby."

Many things seem to end up where they started, and this story is no different. That's one benefit of growing older; you gain the perspective of hindsight. Eventually, if we pay attention, we see how seemingly unrelated events are woven together. Some call it God's plan; others call it fate or dumb luck. Either way, the question becomes: how much control do we really have over our own destiny?

I made arrangements to meet my son Kyle and Kristy here in the city park at nine o'clock this morning. I'm pretty sure Kyle will be on time. Today is the big day, and he is prompt in everything he does. I can see our bank across the street. The big clock on the corner of the building says I still have forty minutes before they arrive. The bank is the 1st Bank of O'Fallon, and the Greenfield family has owned it since 1868. The name is very descriptive since it was literally the first bank in our small town, O'Fallon, located just seventeen miles east of St. Louis, on the Illinois side of the Mississippi river. I suppose our bank is like many old banks in the Midwest. It occupies the corner of the block, indicating its importance among the other businesses as the cornerstone of

commerce in the small town. All the buildings are brown-brick in construction, with storefront windows displaying their goods to those who walk down the wide sidewalks. While most of the buildings are one level, the bank stands two stories, but seems taller with the steep roofline, topped off with the lightning rod. Summertime in O'Fallon can bring vicious thunderstorms with damaging lightning, so a rod is not uncommon on the taller buildings, and a two-story building in O'Fallon is considered a taller building. The rod draws no unwanted attention to the structure, thanks to careful planning many years ago, but more on that later.

To understand why I'm here today, we need to go back to where all this started, four generations ago. Our bank was opened by my great-great-grandfather Levi Greenfield, a few years after he returned home from the Civil War. He managed to escape the war without bodily harm, but it changed his character dramatically. Before the war, Levi was a strong, confident young man who quickly gained rank in the Confederate Army. He was also brash and arrogant, and had few true friends. These characteristics did not conflict with his rank as major, but he found it lonely and many times frightening during the war, unable to share his fears with anyone close. A soldier's life during the Civil War was different in many ways from today's soldier. While both generations faced danger and its associated fear, yesteryear's soldiers had only their fellow troops to lean on for moral support. They didn't have email, instant messaging, video chats and all the communication advances available today via global satellite systems, bringing their families to the battlefield. It was cold and lonely during the Civil War,

especially for men like Levi who kept to themselves.

Levi and his men had fought together for over three years. They were proud and bold warriors during their first two years in combat, but the third year took its toll. More than half their numbers were gone and those remaining grew weary, both physically and mentally. Morale continued to fall with each lost battle. Toward the end of the war, in February 1864, Levi and his remaining troops surrendered to General Sherman at the Battle of Meridian. That battle was fought in Lauderdale County, Mississippi, and was considered a dry-run for Sherman as he prepared to march on Atlanta. After the battle, Confederate prisoners were sent to various Union camps across the northern and southern states. This practice separated soldiers from their commanders and friends, adding to the prisoners' feeling of isolation and defeat. Levi and just a few of his men were sent to a prison camp known as the Louisiana State House, not far from New Orleans. More than a few men died from their injuries and the elements during the long march to the camp. Those who survived the trip considered themselves lucky, until they realized the conditions of the camp.

Each day imprisoned was filled with basic survival activities and prayer that the war would soon end. As with any war, one year in a prisoner of war camp seems an eternity. When the war did end, it was still several more months before Levi and his surviving comrades were finally released. During his captivity, Levi was stripped of his military rank, becoming just another anonymous prisoner in the camp. The conditions were primitive, and prisoners had no civil rights in the 1860's. There was no consideration of the

basic comforts and privileges that our politically correct world now provides. The time spent in the camp had a life-changing effect on Levi, especially one day late in the summer of 1864.

The story passed down through the generations of our family, tells of one night in the prison camp when a tremendous storm blew in. The rain was torrential with frequent lightning exploding in the dark sky. The thunder was a constant roar, louder than cannons on the battlefield. A lightning strike burst one of the prisoners' tents into flames. Levi had been sitting alone but flew into action when he saw the men engulfed in flames, silhouetted by the night's darkness. He grabbed a threadbare blanket and dunked it into an old horse trough used to hold the prisoners' drinking water. He ran toward the danger as others were running from it, smothering the flames on several prisoners who had fled the tent. After everyone outside the tent had been addressed, Levi ran inside and carried out several more prisoners who had been too injured to run from the fire. Somehow, Levi escaped significant burns to himself during the event. Then standing alone in the rain, watching the tent crumble to the ground in flames and smoke, Levi was suddenly struck by lightning and fell to the ground.

Three days passed before he regained consciousness in the prisoners' medical tent. Calling it a medical tent was a joke. It was really just a staging area, where the sick and injured waited to die. Fortunately, the lightning had left Levi relatively uninjured, except for a dramatic burn on his face from the direct strike. The burn went from the edge of his chin up to the bottom of his right temple. Levi was fortunate his mouth, nose, and eyes had not been injured.

Infections to those areas typically meant death in the unclean conditions of the camp. After a few days, Levi was released from the medical tent and returned to his fellow prisoners. His clothes had been completely incinerated by the lightning's impact, so he had to wear the rags gathered for him by those who had seen and heard of his brave actions. Now there was nothing left to show the status Levi had gained as a major. However, from that point on, he held a position much higher than his military rank. He was now friends with his comrades. Out of respect, not military obligation, his new friends simply called him "Major." It was a fitting title for a man who had performed such an unselfish and heroic deed.

When Levi returned home to O'Fallon after the war, he worried how his family would treat him. Many of his friends and family had gone off to fight for the northern states, and they had won the war. How would they accept him now? Because he returned with a newfound love for his family and friends, he eventually became the most respected man in the town of O'Fallon.

Several years after his return, a fellow-prisoner of Levi's appeared in O'Fallon and was surprised to find that no one knew of the Major's heroic actions. However, it didn't take long for Levi's friend to make sure everyone in town knew of his acts. After that, the entire town called him "Major," and did so until the day he died. Levi's simple marble tombstone had his name inscribed as Major Levi Greenfield; not referencing his military achievement, but rather his respect from the entire town of O'Fallon.

It is uncertain exactly how Levi found the means to open the bank, as money was scarce after the war. But his interest in each and

every person who opened an account created loyalty, which built his business quickly. The 1st Bank of O'Fallon, along with Levi's welcoming style of customer service, has been in the Greenfield family ever since.

Each new generation has taken over the business from the previous. My son is the current Chief Executive Officer, taking the reins when I retired fifteen years ago. Kristy doesn't seem interested in following in the family footsteps, not yet anyway. It's funny how quickly things can change though. I think banking and money is in our blood. For example, we've shared a hobby for generations of collecting currency. Not old and valuable coins but just "gently used currency", as we like to call it. We randomly find and save coins and bills that are five to fifty years old, as they circulate through the bank. We like to imagine what it was like for people of that era to hold the money in their hands; on what and how they would spend it. What dreams did they have, that were brought to life by those very bills? We let the younger members of the family play with the money, acting out stories of what it might have been like in those days. Maybe our hobby, and what she will learn today, will be interesting enough to steer Kristy toward working at the bank one day, we will see.

Sitting here waiting on my favorite park bench, a cool breeze just blew by causing me to pull up the zipper on my light jacket. We had our first cold spell of the year and then it warmed again for a brief reprieve. But the pleasant break from the cold is almost over, and we will soon be facing the harsh Midwestern winter common to O'Fallon. It's curious when the weather can't make up its mind

which season it wants to be. "Indian Summer" is a good example. We use the term when the temperature has turned cold and then a few warm days temporarily return. The weather seems to want to go back in time for a while to relive one season before it moves on to the next. Those few days of "Indian Summer" are often appreciated much more than all the warm days during the summer season combined. Some say the term "Indian Summer" came from the white man's distrust of the Native American Indians and was used to refer to the unpredictable and temporary nature of the mild weather, but maybe the term has a deeper meaning. Perhaps it's a term of respect that recognizes the Indians were in tune with the mysteries of nature, and could understand the ebb and flow of the seasons.

It's early November now, and the majority of the leaves are on the ground. Most have already changed from their autumn beauty, to a dried and crisp shell of what they once were; a microcosm of nature's cycle for most living things.

When I walk on the crunchy leaves, I'm immediately taken back to when I was a boy. My father, Joe Greenfield, would rake the leaves into a big pile. Then, my friends and I would jump into the pile and swim through the poky leaves to exit on the other side. My father would re-rake the pile and we would do this over and over again for what seemed like hours. It probably wasn't hours, but it is hard to measure time when recalling a memory.

My childhood was full of fun, well, after the age of ten or so. Previously it was rather ordinary; however, a single event can transform an ordinary time into something magical. I'm sure Levi, my father, and all my ancestors in-between would agree with me.

It's all in how we perceive the everyday events in our lives. Do we see them as ordinary, or as seeds that, when given attention, can grow into something special?

II. **55 Years Ago...**

I was lying in bed, just starting to wake up for the day, sorting through my dreams before they vanished from memory. There was no real reason to wake up now versus in an hour or two. While it was a Saturday, it seemed like any other day. It was mid-July, and I was on summer break from school. Even though it was still relatively early, I could feel the day's heat already warming the east facing window of my bedroom.

I lived with my parents in a big house on North Oak. The owner of the town mill built it in the early 1890's, and it stood as the grand jewel of O'Fallon for several decades. After the mill owner died, the house was turned into a nursing home, but then sat vacant after 10 years of operation. My grandfather eventually bought it back in the early 1940's, soon after my father was born. Years later, my father would somehow find the money to remodel the old house and restore its former glory. When I was a child, it was a bit rundown, but never dirty. My mother made sure it was always clean, and worked hard to make the old house our home.

My days were filled with getting up around ten o'clock, eating a bowl of cereal, and going outside to "play." The year was

1967. I was ten years old and there were no video games, no internet, nor PC's for that matter. We only had three TV channels, with soap operas consuming the air waves during the day. To keep from going completely crazy with boredom, we hung out with our friends, typically outside to give our mothers a break. Sometimes we rode our bikes to the park. Other times we hiked down to the city cemetery, which was pretty neat, although kind of creepy. Mostly we just hung out and didn't do much of anything.

The prolonged boredom from our repetitive daily routine, combined with the summer heat, was sapping the life out of us. It was turning into a self-perpetuating way of life; the less we did, the less energy we had to do anything. Sleeping in late almost became one of the day's events. Even though Nat King Cole's song was four years old, it was still a favorite on the radio and had become our summer anthem: *Those Lazy-Hazy-Crazy Days of Summer.* Each day was much like the day before, and what the next would be, they all just ran together. I would never have admitted it, but in some ways I looked forward to school starting in the fall, just for a change of pace.

As I was lying there in my hazy state, I sprang upright in my bed when a tremendously loud clap of thunder shook our house. I jumped to the window and looked outside, expecting to see a tree on fire from a lightning strike. To my surprise, everything looked normal, except for all our neighbors running outside to inspect their homes. So I wrote it off as a sonic boom, made by the Air Force jets testing the limits of their newest aircraft.

Mach flight started back in 1947, when Chuck Yeager first broke the sound barrier. Now, twenty years later, the jets that flew from nearby Scott Air Force Base were travelling in excess of Mach 3 over the populated area of O'Fallon. I suppose the low flight patterns were some simulation for the ongoing war in Vietnam; but I didn't really care about that then. Booms were a novelty at first to me and my friends, and we enjoyed being present to witness those advancements in technology. We used to play a game to find the jet when we heard a boom. It wasn't easy as the jet was often halfway across the sky by the time we heard it. But as with most novelties, the fun wears off, especially if negative effects happen. They moved the tests to more remote areas after receiving numerous complaints of hearing loss in small children, as well as cracked walls and foundations brought on by the loud, ground shaking noise.

I flopped back down on my bed ready for a quick nap when my father burst into my room like a second clap of thunder. "Bobby, wake up son! Hey, are those eyes open?" With a gentle shake of my shoulder he proclaimed, "Today is going to be our first Family Fun Day."

That got my attention. Sitting up and squinting at him through wincing eyes I replied, "Dad, it's Saturday morning… it's still early." Not that the day of the week really mattered to me, but the clock on my desk told me it wasn't even nine o'clock.

"Come on Buddy… let's go tell Mom… we need to get moving."

While Dad pulled me from my bed, I looked at him as if he'd gone crazy. We literally ran from my room to the living room

where my mother was sewing. She seemed surprised to see him, but ignoring her questioning expression he quickly repeated the announcement. He said he had to go to the bank for a few minutes, and he would hurry back soon. While I must have been standing there with my mouth open, he walked over to me and asked, "Bobby, if you could share an adventure with any of your friends, who would it be?"

It didn't take me long to reply since I had spent the summer nonstop with my two best friends, "Dad, you know it would be Jimmy and Rob. Why? What's up?"

He nodded his head, realizing that may have been a dumb question, "Of course, I should have known. Well, I want you to call them up right now and see if they can spend the day with us. If they can, tell them to be here in an hour, and we'll hit the road."

"To where?" I asked with wide eyes, hoping this wasn't some type of joke.

"That's a secret for now, but get on the phone and I'll be back in about an hour." Dad saw my mother's confused look and he gave her a wink, followed by a little smirk, and then a thunderous laugh.

Dad left in a frenzy and yelled back to us that we should be ready for a full day of fun! My mother and I just stood there looking at each other, but his attitude was contagious and we found ourselves getting excited for the upcoming adventure. I called my friends Rob and Jimmy. Soon we were all sitting in our living room, when Dad came bursting back through the door. His eyes were wide and bright with a shine I don't think I'd ever seen before. He was happy to see

my friends were already there, "Hey boys, glad you could make it. Did Bobby tell you what's going on?"

They both looked at me and then back at my father. Rob said, "Mr. Greenfield, I don't think any of us know what's going on, but we're ready to find out."

Holding the door open, Dad said, "Well, there is only one way to find out, and that way is in the car. Let's go gang."

We didn't know where we were driving, but Dad kept talking and asking us questions during the twenty minute drive to Belleville, the closest "big" town near O'Fallon. When we sensed we may be getting close to our destination, Dad informed us we were going to the annual county fair, about ten miles on the other side of Belleville. I had only heard of the fair from my friends who had been fortunate enough to go with their families. We had never been to the fair; it had always been too hot, too far away, cost too much, etc. There was always a reason not to go.

As we walked toward the fairgrounds, we could see the tops of all the rides and game booths behind the large wooden fence. The backdrop of structures seemed to keep going on and on. When we went through the gates, I could smell all the aromas of fair food: hot dogs, cotton candy, and just about every type of food-on-a-stick imaginable. It was all there. The lights and music from all the rides blended together to form one, overwhelming blur of senses I can only describe as fun. It was just like on TV, or in the movies, when families or even Elvis would go to the fair, but now it was us!

Once inside the gate, the first thing Dad did was walk up to the booth to buy tickets. You had to use tickets for everything: rides,

food, even the Cake Walk. We wanted to do it all, but I knew we would be limited to just a few tickets. Dad was a banker. Most of my friends thought that meant we owned all the money in the bank. What it really meant was our money stayed in the bank, and we didn't spend much at all. I remember Dad telling me many times that money in the bank can earn more money by collecting interest. Then that interest collects interest, which is called compounding interest. The ripple effect of compounding interest is what Albert Einstein called the 8th Wonder of the World. He would tell this to my mother and me like we should be impressed, but it always fell on deaf ears. The real story was we couldn't afford whatever it was we wanted.

Dad walked up to the booth and pulled out a big wad of bills. My mother and I looked at each other and then back at the money. Dad ordered enough tickets for us to have twenty each! He squatted down so his eyes were on our level and instructed us, "Boys, here are your tickets. Use them wisely, but if you run out, just come ask me for more. Now go have fun, and meet us at that hot dog stand in one hour." Rob, Jimmy, and I screamed like little girls as we ran off to whatever awaited us. I looked back to my mother, who was looking rather cross at my father, with her arms folded and her back stiff. Dad didn't care, he just kept joking and laughing, saying, "It's okay Honey, today is Family Fun Day." From that brief glance, I remember my father was tall and had an Elvis look about him, with his dark hair, sideburns, and his sideways grin. And my mother had her circa 1960's sunglasses on, with a scarf over her curly hair, making her look very hip. Maybe we were in an Elvis movie after

all.

My friends and I felt as if we owned the world. After we rode the spinning teacup ride, we needed to take a minute to regain our balance. We decided to walk around the grounds and inventory everything we wanted to do. We had lots of tickets, but we didn't want to use them all on the first rides and games we saw, just to find something better later. So we spent most of the hour just looking around.

When our hour was up, we met my parents at the hot dog stand. Dad excitedly ran up to us. As he hoisted me up in the air and looked me square in the eyes, he asked, "So tell me Bobby, what have you done so far?"

"Well... we rode the teacup ride... took a little break... and then we walked around checking out the other rides." My voice was excited and my eyes wide open.

My father put me down gently, with a surprisingly serious look on his face. Then he regained his full of life composure and told us, "Boys, if you just look around all day, you won't have time to actually enjoy yourselves. You have tickets to a fun day in your hands... all you have to do is use them." Shockingly, Dad actually referred to a Beatles song; I didn't even know he knew who they were. He said, "I know I'm no expert, but when George Harrison sings *Within You Without You*, I think he's saying that it's up to each of us to decide how much 'life' we add within our lives... and if we don't take the time to appreciate every day, our lives will just plod along, without us really participating." He took my mother's hand, and walking toward the hot dog stand asked, "Now, who's hungry?"

While we were having lunch with my parents, my mother told us about all the rides they had ridden, and how it reminded her of when she and my father dated. She had the same look in her eyes as my father now, they shined. After lunch, the five of us stayed together and rode rides, played games, told stories and just had fun the entire afternoon. There were times when we would have to force ourselves to take a rest because our sides hurt from laughing. At the end of the day, we found we hadn't used all our tickets because we spent more time enjoying each other than actually on the rides or playing games. The fair became the backdrop for our fun, rather than the source. As we walked the grounds, the loud speaker played the new Turtles' song *So Happy Together*.

We usually left places early to avoid traffic, but that day we stayed until they turned off the lights, only making it more fun to find our way out in the dark. Rob, Jimmy, and I would run ahead and hide in the shadows, and my parents would pretend they had lost us. While I was hiding, I enjoyed watching my parents holding hands and smiling at each other; something I hadn't seen in a while. I actually shivered with the warm feeling it gave me, to see them *so happy together*. When they would finally find me, we would all roll on the ground, tickling each other and laughing. By then, Rob and Jimmy would run up and jump on the pile of us, and the tickling would take on a new level of fun. Then we would run ahead and do it all over again.

My friends and I were fighting off sleep on the drive home because we didn't want the day to end. We dropped Jimmy and Rob at their houses and then went home. When we walked through our

backdoor into the kitchen my mother asked, "It's late, but does anyone want anything to eat or drink?"

"Hey Mom, I know it is summertime, but can we have some hot chocolate?"

"Well, that's not what I expected, but sure, why not?"

It wasn't cold in July by any means, but I just wanted to drink hot chocolate because it sounded like fun. It was a fitting end to our first, but not last, Family Fun Day. Soon, my eyes couldn't stay open any longer, so my parents tucked me into bed; another treat for me. I heard my door shut with them laughing in the hallway. I heard their door shut, one more giggle, and then silence. My face was sore from all the laughing during the day, but I drifted off to sleep still smiling.

When I think back to my childhood, the day at the fair was the best day of my young life, up to that point anyway. Rob and Jimmy never stopped talking about it. We had ruled the Earth, and our tales recounting the day turned into legend in the small town of O'Fallon; well, with all our friends on the playground anyway. My parents talked about that day, and night, for years to come. It seemed to be as special for them as it was to me, although maybe for different reasons.

III. My Sixteenth Birthday, Where it all Began

Like most kids growing up in 1973, my sixteenth birthday meant only one thing to me: getting a driver's license. I had graduated from after-school Driver's Education, and had spent what seemed like endless hours practicing behind the wheel with my parents. Now it was time to take the official test. I did fine on everything, except parallel parking. My right front bumper just touched the pole causing the red flag to quiver. I couldn't tell if the test-proctor had noticed or how it might impact my result. So I returned to the waiting room and sat with my parents while the proctor reviewed his notes and tallied my score.

While I waited, I noticed people were generally not happy at the Department of Motor Vehicles. I'm not sure why. It seemed they were irritated to spend time in line. What seemed strange to me was they were going to spend this time somewhere, doing something, so why not make the best of it. It was an attitude I think I learned from my father.

After waiting for what seemed an eternity, I was informed that I had passed the test. We had to wait in another line to complete the paperwork and pay the small fee, but this was one line I certainly

did not mind. Standing there with my passing papers in my hand felt like I had a winning ticket to the new Illinois state lottery, and I was waiting to be paid. After taking my picture and getting my license, we dropped Mom off at home and I took Dad to lunch; well, he paid but I drove. The events of the morning were certainly a big milestone to this teenager, but it's what happened in the afternoon that changed my life.

After lunch, Dad took me to the bank. I thought he had some quick work to do, but we walked past his office to the back of the building. We went behind the tellers and the offices. This was a place I had never been, even though I had spent my whole childhood playing all over the bank. I noticed Dad was a bit nervous and kept looking over his shoulder to see if anyone was watching us. In a hushed voice, Dad said, "Bobby, stand here in the hall and tell me if anyone comes."

I whispered, "Dad, what are we doing? Where are we going?" I took my post, although I wasn't sure what I was supposed to be doing.

"Bobby, please son, just keep an eye out while I… there… okay… come here quick."

I turned around to see my father standing in an opening where the wall had stood just a moment ago. It seemed like a scene from a James Bond movie. "Dad, what the heck happened?"

"Come here Bobby and I'll show you. Hurry son."

As I stepped past the open plane where the wall should have been, my father pulled a lever and the wall slid back to its original position. I stood there with my mouth open, not knowing how to

react. I turned to get an explanation from my father, but he had already started walking down the dimly lit, narrow hall. After two bends in the hallway, we came to an abrupt end. I thought it was strange to have a hall that led to nowhere. "Dad, where do we go now?" I asked, almost afraid to know. My father looked at me with a grin and turned to face the left wall. He reached up to an alcove near the ceiling and pulled out an old key. He then felt along the wall until he found a little nub in the paneling, which he slid to the side exposing a keyhole. As the key turned, there was a soft clicking noise. My father gave me a knowing smile and pushed on the wall. A door appeared and opened into a small room, approximately ten feet by ten feet in size.

"Dad, this is way beyond cool. What is this place?"

"Shhh, come in and I'll explain."

We stepped inside without saying another word, as if we were entering church late and didn't want to be noticed. There wasn't much in the room except for a small table, a chair, and a strange-looking statue sitting on the table. It had an odd shape resembling an old timepiece. It wasn't a clock shape, but more of a sundial in fluid motion, as if a wave of time were washing over it. The best I could figure, the statue was made of metal, perhaps bronze. Just by looking at it I could tell it was heavy and also very old. Somehow it looked familiar.

"Son, I know this looks strange, but I think you will find it exciting. I've wanted to bring you here for years now, but I had to wait until you turned sixteen."

"Why?" Was all I could manage to say as my mind tried to

comprehend my surroundings.

"Bobby, this is a long story... have a seat and I'll do my best to explain. It all starts with our ancestor, Levi Greenfield."

"Dad, I already know about Levi... how he had been in a prison camp and was injured there... and how he came back to O'Fallon and opened this bank... but what does that have to do with this hidden room?"

My father smiled and said, "Only a few people in O'Fallon know the whole story, and all those who do are in the Greenfield family. The elder Greenfields wanted to be here with us today, but this is something I selfishly wanted to do myself. This is a long story, but probably the best one you will ever hear."

Dad made himself comfortable leaning against the wall while I sat in the chair at the small table, glued to his every word. It took over an hour for him to recount the extraordinary tale, in a deliberate, rehearsed fashion.

When Levi was on his way home from the war, his travels took him through the small town of Hamburg, Arkansas. He was dirty and worn-out; a far cry from the bold young man with broad shoulders who left for the war only four years ago. Now, his eyes were shallow and never focused on detail, just general shapes. He had just been released from prison camp and still wore the tattered clothing his fellow prisoners had given him. Most people avoided men who looked like Levi. There were many of them, wandering through the countryside trying to make their way home. It was wise to stay clear of these men, as many were unstable and would just as soon hurt you as ask for help.

At the time, Hamburg was small, but it was quickly becoming a major town in the area. The dirt streets were teeming with activity. While Levi was walking through town, trying to politely ask for food, an old Indian woman started to follow him. With every turn down a new street, the old woman followed. After a while, she approached Levi and asked if she could help him. He felt uncomfortable around this woman. She was discreet, so he couldn't tell for sure, but he felt that she was staring at the newly formed scar, still healing from the burn on his face. Levi was desperate, hungry, and tired to be particular, so he followed the old woman back to her house for a meal.

Her home was not what he had imagined it would be. Indians were still considered primitive in the 1860's, and he had expected her to live on the poor side of town. However this woman lived in a modest home on over 100 acres of wooded property just outside town. The house itself was fairly small as she lived alone, but Levi could tell it was well made with quality materials. A house like that, on 100 acres, was typically owned by someone with social and economic standing, not an old Indian woman; but Levi could tell there was something special about this person.

Right away, the old woman made Levi feel at home. She prepared a bowl of hot stew for him while he rested in a comfortable chair. Levi had not eaten meat in over two years, so this was quite an unexpected treat. After he had finished his meal, she allowed him to take a hot bath, his first in a very long time. He couldn't help himself as he fell asleep in the steaming tub. When he woke up, he was in a bed, almost two days later. He never did determine exactly

what had happened during those days, though he reflected on it often during the years that followed. When he looked in the mirror that morning, he noticed his scar had healed dramatically, as if several years had gone by. The old lady said that while he slept, she had applied a compress to his face, just as her Indian ancestors taught her when she was a child. Whatever it was had worked miracles. Levi didn't realize it at the time, but the healing scar mirrored the transformation of his core character.

Unexpectedly, Levi stayed with the old woman for several months. While there, she taught him many of the old Indian ways and customs. She could tell Levi was a man of integrity and was worthy of learning the Indian lifestyle and hearing the ancient stories. During this time, the old woman would check on Levi's scar to ensure it was healing properly. After a while, she was able to persuade him to tell her how he got the scar. Levi was reluctant to share the story, but how could he refuse her after all she had done for him. The story of his heroism only confirmed her impression of his character.

As the weeks passed, they would take walks around her property, which included a small cemetery on a hill not far from her house. In the middle of the cemetery was an incredible Indian "Life Pole." It resembled the totem poles of the Eskimos, and was used in Native Indian cultures to depict the history of many generations within the tribe or a family. Their walks became shorter as the old woman's energy was quickly waning. Levi learned she was ill and dying of what appeared to be simply old age. Having no family left, she seemed to adopt him as her son. Eventually, Levi regained his

strength and had done all he could around the house to make the old woman comfortable for her remaining days. Although he was anxious to return home to his family, Levi could not leave his friend alone in her failing health.

One night, the old woman told Levi she had something to give him. Even though she could barely walk, she made her way over to a table in her living room. She asked Levi to move the table a few feet, aligning the legs with four small marks on the floor. Then, she instructed him to go to the closet to get a carefully wrapped bundle off the top shelf and bring it to the table. Levi almost dropped the package as it was much heavier than its size would indicate. He placed it on the table, where the old woman respectfully removed the wrapping. There were many layers to protect the contents, telling Levi that whatever was inside was indeed valuable. The last layer was pulled back to reveal the odd shaped statue on the table in front of us now.

I couldn't believe the story I was hearing. If it weren't my father telling me, and in this strange room I had never seen, I would not have believed it. Still, I couldn't wait to hear more. I could tell already this was going to be life changing. Dad continued his story, all the time pacing back-and-forth. His energy was a combination of nerves and excitement, but I could see he was being careful to tell the story accurately.

When the old woman gave the statue to Levi, she had an amazing story to go with it. She said the statue had been given to her father from his father, who received it from his father before him. She didn't know exactly how her ancestors came to have it

originally, but it had always seemed to have been with the family. The old woman confided it was difficult to understand the powers of the statue, but basically it allowed the owners to return to days in their past so they could better appreciate them. She stressed to Levi that life is made up of individual days, and each should be considered special. She gave him basic instructions on how to use the statue, but as we found out later, it took Levi's entire life, plus a few generations after, to grasp how to really use it, and we are still learning.

As the old woman was telling this story, Levi could see the life drain from her; this would be her last tale. She had one more important piece of information to tell him. He must find, or build, a tall object to harness the power of the thunderbolt to give power to the statue. The tall object had to be exactly 100 paces from the statue. If he constructed it correctly, the structure would be able to keep track of the days used and those still waiting to be relived. She explained the Life Pole in the cemetery was her tall structure, and it was exactly 100 paces, or 300 feet, from the center of the four marks on the floor in her living room. The table where she had unwrapped the package also had four marks in the center of it to indicate exactly where the statue should be placed on the table. She then told Levi to go to the Life Pole and remove the very top section and take it with him; it was the counterpart to the small statue. He would need both parts to make the statue's power come alive.

As the old woman was growing very weak, she told Levi she had transferred her estate into his name. He should sell it and use the money to do good things for others. With those last words, the

old woman drifted away. It seemed she had a content smile on her face as Levi held her in his arms. She would leave a legacy after all.

The next day, Levi buried the old woman in her family's cemetery. He went into town and worked with Hamburg's lawyer and mayor to sell her property. The town council had been anxious to purchase the property to expand the city limits in preparation for a new sawmill, so the deal went through very quickly. As part of the contract, Levi insisted the cemetery would be preserved just as it was. Before Levi packed up to leave town, he took a marble tombstone to her grave as a lasting tribute to her life. It was something neither weather nor time could destroy.

After he turned from the grave, Levi walked over to the Life Pole. He looked at the carvings differently now. He could see how the images reflected the generations of her family, but there was one figure in all the generations, as if one person was able to appear in each. After making sure he was alone, Levi slowly climbed the Life Pole so he could retrieve the top section; the counterpart to the small statue. It was about twice the size of the statue, but similar in shape and also very heavy. The weight of the object alone kept it on the pole so no tools were required for removal. It was a struggle to carry it down the Life Pole without falling, but Levi managed without incident. He carefully wrapped the top section and placed it in the saddle bag opposite the small statue to balance the weight. Along with the small statue were the proceeds from the sale of the property: $10,000 in gold. At the going rate of $30 per ounce in 1865, that was nearly twenty-five pounds of gold.

I thought Dad would be getting tired by now, with all his

pacing, but he was actually getting more excited as he continued his story.

It took Levi almost four months to make his way back to O'Fallon. Occasionally, he would stop and work odd jobs to get food and a little money to continue his journey. He could have used the gold in his saddlebags, but he had promised the old Indian woman he would use it to help others, not himself.

During his trip home, Levi thought long and hard about what he would do with the rest of his life. While he had plenty of gold, he didn't have land to farm, nor any real education to be a doctor or lawyer. He liked the idea of working with people, since his basic character had changed the day he had been struck by lightning. The long days of traveling gave Levi time to decide he would go into the banking business. He remembered Mike, a man from the prison camp who had been a banker in Memphis. During those endless days, Mike told long stories of the good feelings he had when he could help people save money, and then use their savings to purchase something to really change their lives. Mike also taught Levi about interest, and how it worked both for the bank when it lent money, and for a person when investing their money. Banking was going to be his way to help others, just as he promised the old Indian woman he would do.

Levi finally found himself on the outskirts of O'Fallon. He was afraid how his family would receive him. After all, he had left such a mean and bitter man. Plus, he had gone off to defend the South when most of his family and friends supported the North and their anti-slavery ideals. Even though Levi never owned slaves, he

had viewed them as a commodity before the war, not as people. He had come to realize his decision to defend the South was partly out of sheer defiance of his family. He had always loved his family, but there were times when he used his arrogance and physical stature to force his opinion on others. The war was just another opportunity to demonstrate his superiority, and picking the unpopular side was his typical tactic. His views were changed now, but would his family welcome him back?

Levi hitched his horse at the end of his parents' drive and walked up the path leading to the open kitchen door. He could hear his mother in the kitchen preparing dinner. The smell of her cooking took him back to when he was young. He had always enjoyed his mother's cooking, but now realized it was another thing he had taken for granted. He had not eaten in two days, and his stomach was making audible noises when he walked through the door. It took just an instant for his mother to recognize him and for all his fears of rejection to disappear. Levi's mother dropped the dish she was holding and ran to him. She grabbed him like she would never let go and screamed out for Levi's father to come. Levi was now nervous again, as it was really his father's opinion that would determine his acceptance. His father opened the door thinking his wife had been burned or injured based on her screams; but when he saw Levi, he understood. They stood there for a few moments and didn't say a word. Then, as a tear rolled down the old man's age-cracked cheek, Levi's father embraced him. Levi felt just as he did when he was a small boy, when his father would hug him and make him feel safe from all the dangers in the world. In those moments, Levi

remembered what the old Indian woman had told him about traveling back in time. Between his mother's cooking and his father's embrace, he wondered if this was what she had been talking about. Perhaps time travel was more of an emotion or a feeling than a physical transformation. Until he could use the statue, he wouldn't know for sure.

Levi was an only child, like all of the Greenfields, but his parents' house was soon filled with friends, all there to welcome him home. He briefly told them of his war experiences, his time in prison camp and his ordeals traveling back home. He swore he would never leave again, and he kept his promise.

It took time for Levi to pursue his dream of opening a bank in O'Fallon. Times were still hard from the war, and money was scarce. He had to be careful not to reveal the gold all at once, as he would be suspected of stealing. It was not unusual for soldiers to return home with stolen items taken from ransacked homes. But he worked hard over the next two years, and the doors of the 1st Bank of O'Fallon evidentially opened. By the end of the first day, he had eight customers. Levi's business steadily grew over the next few years as his reputation as being fair and honest spread throughout the area. By the end of his fifth year in business, he had remodeled the bank and hired additional staff.

No one knew what Levi had been up to, but he had been searching for years to find a way to build the tall structure needed to capture the power of the lightning bolt, to make the statue work. He decided to commission a man to build a tall clock to stand in the lobby of his bank, with the statue's counterpart integrated into the

design of the top crown. When the clock was brought in, everyone was impressed with its size and the obvious quality of the workmanship, it kept perfect time. Levi knew that it could not capture the power of lightning sitting inside the lobby, so he had a local blacksmith install a lightning rod on the roof of the bank. The rod was grounded in the earth as normal, but it also had a hidden wire connected to the small statue's counterpart, now affixed to the top of the large clock. This would provide protection to the building from the many summer thunderstorms, and also feed the tall structure the necessary power to work along with the mysterious statue in front of us now. To accommodate the 300-foot requirement between the statue and its counterpart on the clock, Levi had to purchase the adjoining building and do extensive remodeling of the bank. During the remodeling and expansion of the bank, he had this small, hidden room built. Four marks were engraved on the floor of the small room, which aligned perfectly with the legs of the table where I now sat. The statue sat on the table with its corners touching four small marks on the table; all just like the fabled setup in the old Indian woman's house. The center of the statue was exactly 300 feet from the top of the new clock.

Dad bent and straightened his leg as if he was getting tired of standing. "Dad, how about you sit here for a while and I can stand?" I offered.

"No thanks son, I think better on my feet. Besides, I've been waiting a long time to tell this story. My adrenaline can carry me for a while longer."

Dad went on to tell me that no one in our family knows what

Levi's first attempt to save a day was used for, but we do know what events took place that day. It was a bright sunny day in late May, and Levi decided it would be a good day to save for use in the future. He called it banking a day, like he was depositing a day to be used later. So he followed the instructions the old woman had given him back in her home in Hamburg. He put his hand on the statue and said the words just as she had instructed. It was in the ancient Indian language, so he didn't know exactly what the words meant, only that they would bank the day when the phrase was spoken.

When Levi had finished the phrase, lightning struck the rod on the bank's roof and sent a wave of electricity to the clock. The resulting thunder shook the bank, as the barriers of time had been breached. Just at that moment, the clock's hands spun wildly and suddenly stopped at 11:59. Levi fell to the floor, unconscious for the rest of the day. When he woke up the next morning and returned to the lobby, he found everyone had been worried about him since they didn't know his whereabouts, and they told him what had happened to the clock.

It now made sense to me, as the old clock had never kept correct time in all the years I've been alive. "Hey Dad, do you remember how your dad used to tell people the clock did show the correct time, twice a day?"

"That's right Bobby" Dad replied with a chuckle. "That was his way of deflecting attention from the old clock... but eventually he had to install the clock outside on the street, to appease our customers' complaints about the broken clock in the lobby." Dad took a short mental break, but quickly continued the story so he

wouldn't lose momentum.

It took our ancestors a few Banked Days to figure out how the clock tracked banked and used days, but it is really quite simple. Dad told me that while most people focus on the numbers on the clock, we were really interested in the 60 marks on the clock that typically represent the minutes. He knew this might get confusing, so Dad pulled out a piece of paper and a pen, to diagram how the clock worked as he continued the story.

When a day is banked, the minute hand moves backwards, or counter clockwise one mark from its previous position. So when Levi banked the first day, the clock first reset with both hands pointing directly up to the number twelve. Then the minute hand moved backwards one mark. The time on the clock looked to be 11:59 since the hour hand had not moved and was still pointing straight up. When a Banked Day is used or cashed-in, the minute hand resets clockwise one mark, indicating there is one less day banked and pending use. Also, the hour hand moves clockwise one mark to show one more Banked Day was used. So when Levi used his first Banked Day, the minute hand moved back to the number 12 and the hour hand move one mark clockwise. It then looked like noon, but just a little off since the hour hand was not exactly on the number 12. This is how our tall structure tracks Banked Days waiting to be relived and the days already relived, just as the old Indian woman had predicted.

I was now full of so many questions I thought my head would burst. Dad could sense my state by the way I was fidgeting in my seat. He laughed and asked me if I had any questions. I was

about to jump up and start blurting them out when he stopped me. "Bobby, there have been four generations of Greenfields before you who have had the privilege to use the powers of the statue, and they had many questions too. Over the generations, the answers to those questions have formed the "rules" of the statue. If you learn those rules, I'll bet many of your questions will be answered."

Then Dad leaned back against the wall, told me to turn around, and started reading the rules engraved in the hard wall behind me:

Rules for Using the Statue:

1. Only direct blood descendents of Levi Greenfield can use the statue

2. Each Greenfield descendent can bank up to three days during their lifetime

3. Any unbanked and unused days will be forfeited upon death

4. If anyone outside the Greenfield bloodline is told about the statue, all Banked Days will be forfeited and the power of the statue will end forever

5. Only the last person in the Greenfield bloodline to bank a day can pass the power of the statue to someone in another bloodline

6. A day should not be banked to deliberately cause anyone physical, emotional or financial harm

7. A person must be at least sixteen years old to bank a day

The handwriting on the wall seemed to change for the next rules

8. A person's Banked Days have to be at least one year apart from each other.

9. Concentrate on the specific Banked Day to be withdrawn, so the correct day is selected

The handwriting on the wall seemed to change again for the last rule.

10. A day must not be banked to make someone fall in love with you.

As I thought about each of the rules, I wondered what had happened to prove the rule one way or another. I was sure each rule had an interesting story in itself.

"Dad, have you used any of your Banked Days yet?"

"Bobby, that's a story for another day. I'm afraid I've about lost my voice from all the talking, and I'm pretty sure you've heard enough to keep your mind busy for a while. Besides, we better start heading home soon before your mother thinks you crashed the car on your first day with your license."

I tried to give him a stern look for that remark, but ended up laughing instead. The laugh helped break the tension brought on by Levi's story, and this incredible gift my family had been given. As I was standing up from the table, Dad said, "Now son, this is going to be difficult, but you can't tell anyone about this or it will all come to an end... and unfortunately, that includes your mother."

"Why can't I tell Mom, she's in our family?"

"The rule handed down by the old Indian woman was very

specific Bobby. Only those directly in the bloodline can know of the gift. Mom married into the Greenfield family, so she isn't in the bloodline."

It seemed like a terrible secret to keep from her, but I had no choice.

Before we left the room, Dad told me to use my three days carefully. They are a gift beyond earthly value. He suggested I wait at least a year to bank a day so I would have time to give it real consideration. He said that if I had any questions to feel free to ask him, but be absolutely certain no one is around to hear the conversation and potentially end the power of the statue.

Dad then led us out of the room, locked the door, hid the key, and we returned to the bank lobby. We stood in front of the large clock, and I just imagined all the stories it could tell. Then I noticed two things. First, the top of the clock had an odd crown-like design that was a perfect match to the shape of the statue in the hidden room 300 feet away. It was the counterpart to the small statue. The craftsman who built the clock had done a masterful job blending the design of the clock to fit the statue's counterpart. I knew I had seen that design somewhere before when I first saw the small statue. I figured the wire to the lightning rod was connected to the back of the counterpart, but it was completely concealed.

The second observation was the time on the clock. The current "time" the big clock told was roughly two o'clock. The minute hand was pointing to the 59th mark, and the hour hand was pointing to the 10th mark. I could see how it might look confusing when the minute and hour hands didn't align perfectly to reflect

typical time. Those who might have noticed probably just wrote it off to the broken nature of the old clock. However, it was actually keeping a perfect account of the times our family used the statue.

When we arrived at Dad's car he asked me if I wanted to drive. I would have jumped at the opportunity a few hours ago, but now I felt too tired. After months of anticipation, it turned out that getting my license wasn't the most important event to happen on my sixteenth birthday after all.

\#

An Intersecting Path:

"I'm worried about Frank. I've known him since junior high, and he's in trouble now. Since he returned from the war, he's been distant and restless. I would follow Frank into hell, and I believe I did, but I can't reach him now. I'm afraid he will do something reckless and hurt himself... and maybe others as well. If that wasn't enough, I can't stand my guilt... it's tearing at me every second of every day. Sometimes I think I should just tell Frank and get it out in the open, but I know that would send him over the edge. We both changed in that damned war. I wish we could go back to the way things were before. Anyway, this just isn't the Frank I grew up with. I'll be there for him till the end... I just hope that isn't coming soon."

\#

IV. A Long Year of Walking Forward, and Back

The year after my sixteenth birthday seemed to last forever.

Sure I did all the normal things a sixteen-year-old would do
in the 1970's. I drove my parents' car while working a part-time job
at the local movie theater, trying to save up $1,200 to buy my own
set of wheels. I also developed an interest in girls, although not with
any real success. However, unlike all other sixteen-year-olds, I
spent a lot of time trying to figure out the best strategy for using the
three days I could bank.

I have to admit my first ideas were pretty childish, like going
back to retake a test I had failed, but now knowing all the correct
answers. I thought about using a Banked Day to play a joke on my
friends by mysteriously knowing a trivial thing that happens in the
future; but instinctively I realized that I had to be responsible with
these days.

I think having three Greenfield generations watching over me
added to my sense of responsibility. My father Joe, Grandfather
Frank, and Great-Grandfather Raymond were all still alive and they
all loved me dearly, but keeping track of the nicknames that
addressed their position in the family was confusing to me when I

was young. So my father decided we should simplify the naming convention. They were all to be called "G-Pa" followed by their first name. Many years later, it would be one of the best days of my life when I finally became a G-Pa.

Every now and then, I would ask my father and my G-Pas questions concerning our gift. When I did, I always tried to take possible solutions with me every time. I wanted to show them I was taking this responsibility seriously. That sometimes took a real effort. They say teenage boys think about girls around 90% of the time. Throw in thinking about our gift, and it's a wonder I had enough brain capacity left to function in society.

One summer day, when I was thinking back on our first Family Fun Day at the fair, I almost wrecked my parents' car when I had a realization: that day wasn't a normal day in our family's life, not up to then anyway. Then I remembered the loud clap of thunder when I was waking up that morning. Things were adding up.

So in the evening, I asked my father to go for a walk so we could be alone. It was the first of many walks we would share. When we were far away from anyone, I said, "Dad, I think I've figured something out… something about the old clock at the bank."

The look on my father's face told me he was ready to address any question or theory I might have. "Okay Bobby, what's on your mind?"

"On my sixteenth birthday, I remember how the hour hand on the clock was on the 10th mark, and the minute hand was pointing to the 59th mark. So here is my theory: there have been four generations of Greenfields to use their three banked days. I have to

assume Levi and his son, G-Pa-Raymond, have both used their three Banked Days...so that accounts for six of the ten marks indicated by the hour hand on the clock... that leaves you and G-Pa-Frank to make up the remaining four days... which means both of you have used at least one of your Banked Days. I'm pretty sure you used one of your Banked Days was when we had our first Family Fun Day at the fair when I was ten years old. Also, since the minute hand is on the 59th mark, there is one day banked but unused by either you or G-Pa-Frank... and my guess is it belongs to G-Pa-Frank, but I'm not sure."

"Wow... that was a mouthful... and all very good deduction... but what makes you think I used a Banked Day when you were ten?"

"Your jubilant behavior that day just wasn't like you back then, and I heard loud thunder that morning, just before you came into my room."

Dad stopped and looked at me with pride. He said, "Bobby, your theory makes my head spin... and it's mostly correct. Someone does indeed have one Banked Day yet to use, but I won't tell you who it is or when he banked it. You'll just have to learn those details as they play out."

"Okay, I can accept that... but Dad, can you at least tell me why you banked that day when I was ten? What did it mean to you? I guess I'm trying to figure out what makes a day a good day to bank."

Dad found a place to sit and confided in me, "Bobby, we had all been in a rut. You were bored with summer vacation. I was

getting bored with my job, and it felt like I was stuck in O'Fallon."

His statement surprised me, "I know O'Fallon can get old, but how could you be bored knowing you had this gift?"

"Well, I hadn't used any days yet and I guess it didn't seem real." Then my father looked at me as if he was trying to determine if I was mature enough to hear the rest of the story. Slowly he continued, "I'm very embarrassed to admit this son, but my eyes were starting to wander to other women."

That did catch me off-guard. Finally I said, "What happened?"

"Nothing, I swear I never acted on those thoughts… but I still feel guilty I had them, even now after all these years." After a pause, he continued, "Anyway, your mother seemed content being a housewife, but I sensed she was also becoming bored with O'Fallon."

It was difficult to hear about my parents' issues, even if they were years ago. However, this was something I could tell weighed heavy on my father's heart, so I was determined to be mature and let him speak his mind.

"I remember there was a new song on the radio by Three Dog Night, called *One*. Every time I heard it, I became a little more depressed. It spoke about loneliness and how it can consume your life, whether you're single… or even if you are in a relationship, it can just happen. I don't know… it seemed to nail what we were going through. So instead of spending my time just thinking about the past, I decided to bank one of those days to relive in the future. I thought our situation might somehow seem better to me later... or

maybe banking the day could even help our relationship somehow... but it didn't help... not at first anyway. I got into a lot of trouble with your mother... she was furious when I went missing without any explanation."

"Why? How long does it take to bank a day?"

"When you bank a day you end up staying in the hidden room at the bank the whole day, because you can't live one day twice. We say we 'relive' a Banked Day, but we are really living it for the first time."

Continuing his story, "Just a few years later, I decided to make my withdrawal. I was already missing those days when you were younger, and I was worried about your mother. She seemed to be growing more and more disinterested in me, and if I'm being honest, I guess I was feeling the same way. So on the day I decided to withdraw the Banked Day, I went to the bank early in the morning. Before I knew it, I was back in our house, years ago. The loud clap of thunder you heard when you were waking up that day was the statue and the clock bringing me back to 1967. It took me a while to figure out what had happened... but once I did... I couldn't get enough packed into the day. There was an urgency I had never felt before... like each second in that day was a quick breath of air to a suffocating man. At first I couldn't slow down and I'm sure I looked frantic. Eventually I realized I was there for the whole day and I could relax and enjoy it... but even then, I didn't want to waste one minute."

It was fascinating to hear the details of how the process worked from his perspective, matching his details to my memories.

Dad told me the day after he returned to the future time, my mother said she had a dream about their day at the fair. She said it was so vivid; it was as if she had relived that entire day. It had been a reminder of sorts to all those involved because I too remembered having the same dream, years after our day at the fair. What really mattered though was his relationship with my mother had changed dramatically from the day at the fair forward. She had rediscovered the love they shared when they first married. Dad later found old cards and letters she had written him during the years after that day, they were full of love and genuine interest in him. He stopped thinking of her as just my mother and remembered what she was like when they were dating. He mentally started calling her by her name, Sheila. The attention he had shown her at the fair turned things around for my parents before they had gone on a downward spiral.

Dad reminded me that the events of the day are real back when they happen; it's not a dream that doesn't make any difference. We have to be very careful what we do when we go back, because our actions have a ripple effect on how subsequent events will play out over time. We have to do all we can to make sure those ripples are positive and not harmful in any way. He called those ripples the interest we collect on the Banked Day. It's one thing to just withdraw the money or time you have deposited. The added bonus was the interest you receive. In the case of banking days, the interest is how those days affect other people. As the ripple effect continues and affects others in turn, the net result is compounded interest.

Time passed quickly as we continued to discuss the ripple effect. Finally we noticed it was getting dark, and quickly made our

way home before Mom would start to worry about us. I think we had both shared enough for one walk.

#

A few weeks passed before Dad and I took our next walk, but my thoughts on the subject were constant. I felt as if I was trying to understand the rules of a complicated game that had just been explained to me. The more I understood one rule, the more questions I had. It was my nature not to simply accept a rule as fact. Instead, I wanted to understand what led up to the rule, what would happen if the rule was broken, why the rule existed in the first place. I felt there was still much we had to learn about our gift. The next time we were on a walk, I asked, "Dad, do you know of any times when something went wrong while reliving a Banked Day?"

"Bobby, so far I've tried to focus on the good that Banked Days can bring... but you're smart enough to realize that bad things can happen if we aren't careful. I think you are old enough now to hear this story, about your grandfather. He and I have talked about sharing this with you when the time was right, so I know he won't mind, but please keep an open mind and don't judge him. We decided to share this with you so you won't go down the same path."

Dad told me it started back in the early 1940's. It was actually the spring of 1942. Pearl Harbor had been bombed by the Japanese the previous December, and the United States had joined the Allies in WWII. My grandfather, G-Pa-Frank, was nineteen years old, but mature beyond his years. His mother Peggy had died while giving birth to him, so Frank grew up with just his father, G-Pa-Raymond, who was Levi's son. Frank felt an obligation to stay

and help his father with the bank, but he knew he had to do his duty. He would join the Army and defend his country like his father had done in WWI. Frank was engaged to Dorothy, the only daughter of the owner of the local Five & Dime store, who was also a big client of the bank. Just before Frank shipped out for boot camp, he banked a day. He didn't know if he would survive the war, but if he did, he knew he would want to go back to a time before his world changed as a result of the horrible things he would likely see at war. Soon Frank shipped out for boot camp at Fort Sam Houston in San Antonio, Texas. It was only April, but it was hotter than any summer day he had ever experienced in O'Fallon. It was almost a relief when he was finally sent to Europe.

Frank spent his first two years overseas in harsh combat. In late-May 1944, he knew something big was going to happen. Troops were being maneuvered to support what is now known as D-Day. It was the invasion of Normandy, June 6, 1944, and Frank was in the second wave of troops to land on the beachhead. That day and the following months were horrific, but they led to the end of the war. Frank was fortunate to physically survive the war, but returned to O'Fallon a different man. Unfortunately, his transformation was not positive like it had been for Levi.

He was living with his parents, back in his familiar bedroom, and yet his world had indeed changed. Frank never spoke much of that day on the beach, other than one night when he had nightmares of the landing. That night he cried in his sleep while dreaming of the horrors of stepping on the bodies of his friends lying in the surf during his run to the beach. When he awoke, he found his mother

holding him; he was completely drenched in sweat as if he had just been in the surf. She tried to comfort him, but he felt embarrassed and pretended to fall back to sleep. Frank became withdrawn and disinterested in everything he found in O'Fallon, including Dorothy.

His best friend Claude tried to cheer him up. Having also survived the war, Claude was now studying to become a dentist. Three months after Frank joined the military, Claude turned eighteen and also signed up with the Army. He could have chosen any branch of the military, but he wanted to follow in Frank's footsteps; but even Claude couldn't help Frank now with his depression. As a last resort, Frank decided he should just move away from O'Fallon. He thought if he changed scenery and moved to where no one knew him, somehow things might be better.

Then Frank remembered his Banked Day. He decided to go back to enjoy that day before the war, and then he would move away from O'Fallon. At first, Frank enjoyed himself back in 1942. The town was just as he remembered. With each fond memory he relived, he seemed to let go of the bad ones he gained from the war. Frank was feeling good when he happened upon Claude in the Five & Dime. Claude looked so young sitting at the soda fountain bar talking with Dorothy. Frank was about to run up and talk to his old buddy, when he noticed Claude and Dorothy were acting like they were a bit more than just friends. Claude then leaned forward and gave Dorothy a kiss. Frank's blood boiled at the sight of his best friend kissing his fiancée. Frank did end up running to his old friend, but it was to deliver a violent tackle, which sent them both to the floor exchanging blows. Dorothy's father ran from the back

room when he heard the fight, but didn't arrive before damage had been done to the store and to Claude's face. Frank still carried the skills learned from his training in hand-to-hand combat, and his instincts had kicked in during the fight. Claude would also learn those skills, but in this fight he had no chance. Fortunately for Frank and Claude, Dorothy's father was able to break up the fight before Claude was seriously injured. Frank immediately called off the engagement and left for boot camp the next day.

My grandfather's Banked Day ended and he returned to 1946, after the war. While he walked around the next day, he pieced together what had happened on and after his Banked Day. He now remembered Claude had decided to join the Marines after their fight, and he had been killed in combat in the Pacific theater. Previously, Claude would have joined the Army, and would have been deployed to a different location, avoiding the bullet which had killed him. No one but Frank knew of Claude's other path, and in his isolation Frank was more distraught than ever. That night Frank went to a bar, got drunk, and started to walk home. Frank was not a drinker, so he was easily affected by the alcohol. While he stumbled down the sidewalk, Claude's sister, Carolyn, noticed him and drove up to see if she could give him a ride. Carolyn had never blamed Frank for Claude's death, because she never knew Claude would have joined the Army if they had not fought in the store. Carolyn took Frank to the local diner to sober him up, rekindling their friendship over coffee and pie.

Over the next few months, Carolyn helped Frank remember who he really was. It wasn't long until their relationship grew and

they were married. In just a few years, Carolyn gave birth to my father Joe, and the rest is the history I have always known. Of course, I had known about my grandparents, but I never knew of Claude or this entire story. My history was based on a foundation that had been changed that day back in 1942.

Dad then reminded me to be very careful when living a Banked Day. The ripple effect of those days can be both good and bad. It was good that my grandfather fell in love and married my grandmother, but Claude was dead, and Dorothy ended up moving to Texas.

The day after my walk with my father, I decided to contact my old friends Rob and Jimmy. I wanted to know how they remembered the day at the fair now. Both had the exact same memory. They had a dream the next day in what was future-time. The memory of how they felt that day was so vivid to them that they smiled for weeks. While that day was a blessing to all of us, my father's warning gathered strength. The outcomes from a Banked Day are real, and while they can result in good, they can also be dangerous.

#

A few months later, I was on a walk with Dad and G-Pa-Raymond, albeit a slow walk since G-Pa-Raymond was getting up there in years. G-Pa-Raymond shared another family secret. He told me it is important we only use cash when we go back to a Banked Day.

"Bobby, when you are back in a day from another time, you can't depend on any type of credit. You might try to use a credit

card and find out the bank had not even opened yet. Or if you go back far enough, that type of technology could still be years away. But the main reason we stick to cash is we just can't predict the outcome of how adding debt to ourselves in the past will affect us in the future. We could inadvertently cause a negative financial ripple effect that may have long lasting and devastating results." Then he smiled at me and said, "Why do you think we collect and play with old currency?"

"Well, I guess I thought it was just a game we played. I don't know. I suppose I've never really thought about if there was a bigger reason."

"We use the old currency when we go back in time, when we live a Banked Day. It's the only payment mechanism that doesn't become outdated... but we have to be careful to select the appropriate currency for the year we are returning to. It's alright if the bills are older but we wouldn't want to take money with a newer date than the Banked Day; otherwise, it would be considered counterfeit. We can't risk putting ourselves in jail over such a simple error."

"I've never thought about it before, but I guess you do need some spending money, just to get around and survive for the day."

"Yep, you would be surprised what a difference just a few dollars can make. Here is another question for you Bobby, why do you think we used the old currency to play games with the children in our family?"

"At the time G-Pa, I thought it was just a game to play... but thinking about it now, I guess it was to teach us kids about the value

of money in past times... like the time we played grocery store, and we bought things like a loaf of bread. You were the cashier and said it only cost fifteen cents. That was surprising since a loaf of bread cost around a dollar eighty-nine at the time."

"That's right, it is a good lesson for the children, but it was actually to help the adults remember the value of money in past times. Many years can go by before we use the Banked Day, and we can forget the price of things in the past. It would seem very strange to the checkout clerk if I tried to pay two dollars for that loaf of bread, or if I tried to pay for a tank of gas with a twenty dollar bill when it only totaled three dollars, like it did when I was your age. When you are living a Banked Day, you don't want to draw unnecessary attention to yourself Bobby, especially when it comes to money. Before you know it, someone gets suspicious of the man who is throwing money around. Then you end up spending the rest of your day answering questions. Plus, the version of you who stays there the next day, then has to deal with the result. You want to keep things normal while you are living a Banked Day, so it stays normal in the past, after you return to the future."

I never grew tired of hearing advice from G-Pa-Raymond. It was like having a conversation with a living history book. Sometimes now, I wish I'd used a Banked Day to relive a discussion on one of our walks. I didn't fully appreciate him until it was too late.

#

Dad and I enjoyed several more walks during the winter, and when January came around, the whole country was focused on it

being 1976, our county's bicentennial anniversary. I found it interesting that the United States was less than one hundred years old when Levi was born in 1843. It made me realize and appreciate how long our gift had been in our family. Dad and I spent several walks discussing what we thought might have been the history of the statue before the Greenfields took possession. Our curiosity of the statue's history was starting to consume the conversations on our walks.

While on spring break of my senior year in high school, we decided to take a road trip. We would leave on the first week of summer break and go to where it all started: Hamburg, Arkansas, where Levi met the old Indian woman. We wanted to discover any new details we could about Hamburg and the power of the statue. It was time to stop talking about our history, and time to go explore what was physically left of it in Hamburg.

#

An Intersecting Path:

"When I met Joe, I knew right away he was the man I'd marry and have a family with. We did marry, and we had a beautiful son... but as close as our little family is, I feel there is something my men are keeping from me. At first, I resented being left out of their conversations... but now I've come to accept there is a bond, or something incredibly strong between them that I'm just not part of. I can't imagine it would be anything illegal or dishonest, but we are in the banking business, and sometimes I worry. I guess I'm as much to blame as anyone since I cast a blind eye when extra money just appears. I have to believe in Joe's integrity, even though our early years were a bit rocky."

#

V. Trip for Lost details

While I was preparing for my finals that semester, it was difficult to not think about our road trip, and to instead concentrate on my studies.

Finally, the semester was over and we would be on the road the next day. We had six days before graduation, so there was just enough time to make a quick trip. However, it took some fast talking to convince my mother that this was a good time to leave. After all, why now? Couldn't it wait until after graduation? The truth that we were too excited to wait was not an option, so I came up with an excuse that involved seeing a bicentennial exhibit in Little Rock, which was about to be moved to Chicago. It sounded rather lame as soon as it left my lips, but there was no taking it back at that point. Dad tried to reinforce my story, but only made it worse. Finally, Mom just decided to drop the subject. It's never been easy keeping her out of the loop. I know she gets suspicious; Dad and I just aren't very good at lying. Nevertheless, we were now set for our adventure.

Hamburg is located about 125 miles from Little Rock, Arkansas, two travel days from O'Fallon. The first day was filled

with the normal settling in process of a road trip: making sure we had our snacks and maps, and finding interesting places to stop along the way. On the second day, things slowed down enough for us to drift back into the kind of discussions we would normally have on our walks. It was mid-morning on the second day of our trip when I asked Dad to talk about the rules he mentioned to me on my sixteenth birthday. I asked him how exactly the rules were developed. He told me many were discovered by trial and error. I pressed Dad for more details. There had to be at least a few good stories about how the rules came to be. We certainly had time as we roared down the highway at fifty miles per hour.

Dad smiled, adjusted his hands on the steering wheel and started his story with the same tone in his voice I've heard many times.

"Son, several of the rules were passed on to Levi by the old Indian woman. Those rules mainly focused on who could bank days and how many a person received. She also stressed that the secret of the statue had to be kept within the bloodline or it would all end... and I think the last rule she told Levi was how the power of the statue could be passed from one bloodline to another, just as she passed it to him when she was dying."

"I figured those were passed to Levi from the Indian woman, but how did the other rules come about?"

"Well, some of the other rules were considered to be just good judgment. For example, you shouldn't use a Banked Day to deliberately harm anyone. That was based on the integrity of the Greenfield family, starting with Levi and carried on by each

generation. Levi was smart enough to realize this power could be used for evil purposes, and he was intent it wouldn't happen; not within his bloodline anyway."

"Evil purposes? I'd never even considered using this gift for something evil... but I can see how it could happen. I guess that's why the Indian woman didn't give Levi the power until she was sure he was worthy of it." Over the next few years, I would catch myself thinking about evil ways to use the power. Having those thoughts would make me feel nervous, but I wrote it off as human nature.

Dad continued driving as he told me a new story involving Levi. Another rule was developed early in the Greenfield's tenure with the statue. Levi had married a young lady named Annabel, not long after opening the bank. Unfortunately, she was unable to have children. It was an ironic twist that Annabel's condition would stop the gift of the statue from being handed down to future generations; but as fate would have it, she contracted a disease and died in her late forties. Levi loved Annabel deeply and it took him years to recover from his grief. Eventually he met and married his second wife, Edmona. She was seventeen years Levi's junior and was able to give him a son, my G-Pa-Raymond, when Levi was in his mid-50s. Levi was so eager to teach his son Raymond about the statue, he introduced him to it when Raymond was only twelve years old. Over the next few years, Raymond would try to use the statue but it simply would not work for him. This greatly concerned Levi. At first he questioned if his memory was rusty since he had long ago used his last banked day. Had he forgotten the ancient Indian words or did something else go wrong along the way? Then he started

wondering if he had misunderstood the old Indian woman regarding future generations. Levi thought he might be the end of the Greenfield bloodline after all, and started wondering if his wife had conceived his son by another man. Fortunately, Raymond kept trying and eventually it worked for him. Levi concluded the magic age was sixteen, so ever since, future generations of Greenfields were told about the statue on their sixteenth birthday, to avoid unsuccessful early attempts. It also made sense to wait to make sure the next generation was mature enough to be responsible with the power.

"Dad, I can tell you now that I wouldn't have been able to handle this gift any earlier than when you told me. As it was, my first ideas on how to use a Banked Day were pretty childish. I'm glad you told me to wait at least a year. Actually, I still don't think I'm ready to use one. There's a lot of responsibility that comes with these days... it's not for kids. I'm just grateful to you and my G-Pas... that you all went before me and figured out the rules... that couldn't have been easy."

Dad let out a breath and said, "When you don't know what you're doing, it's hard to get your hands around something as unique as this gift. Trial and error is never easy and seldom fun, but eventually it provides results."

Dad then told me the other rules that were discovered from failed attempts. Years after G-Pa-Frank used his first Banked Day, before WWII, he tried to bank his third day only ten months since banking his second. He put his hand on the small statue, spoke the Indian phrase to bank the day, but nothing happened. He tried again,

thinking he had misspoken the phrase, but still nothing happened. Afraid he had wasted his last two days, he ran out to the bank lobby and checked the clock. Neither hand had moved. A few months later, G-Pa-Frank tried again to bank a day and it worked normally. So he and his father concluded Banked Days must be at least one year apart.

Then a few years later when G-Pa-Frank withdrew a day, he didn't concentrate on the day he wanted to return to when he spoke the Indian phrase. He planned to withdraw the most recent day he had banked, but ended up back in the time of his second Banked Day. It took him a while to understand what had happened regarding when and where he was. Fortunately he realized some of his money was too new before spending any, but he was left with little useable cash. He made the best of the day by visiting friends and family, but the day wasn't what it could have been had he been prepared.

We had been driving for a few hours, so Dad stopped the car at a rest area and suggested we stretch our legs. We got out of the car and went for a short walk. After we left the parking area he said the rule based on the most significant event was definitely the last rule on the wall: to not use a Banked Day to make someone fall in love with you.

"Actually Bobby, I was the one who learned that lesson and wrote the last rule. I'll tell you how it happened, but only if you promise not to think less of me. This is a hard story for a father to tell his son."

Of course I agreed. "Dad, you know I love and respect you.

There's nothing you could have done in your past that will change that... you can tell me... please do, so I don't make the same mistake." I knew if I put it that way, he would tell me.

We were now back near the car, so we sat down on the bench under a lean-to structure, built to provide shade on hot summer days like this. Removing his sunglasses, Dad slowly continued his story. "Bobby, first I have to apologize to you. I told you once that my first Banked Day was when we went to the fair. Actually, it was well before that, and the result of that day has haunted me ever since."

It turns out my father had dated a girl named Cindy before he met my mother. They met late in high school, and he thought he loved her. After a few months of dating, he could tell she was not as interested in him as he was in her. He was eighteen and had already learned about banking a day. So he decided to use his first Banked Day, and if things didn't work out with Cindy, he could come back and fix whatever it was that ended their relationship. Just as he suspected, they did eventually break up; but before he withdrew the Banked Day, he met my mother and their relationship quickly started to grow. They dated through college and got married right out of school, having me soon after.

For years, he didn't even think about the Banked Day, but when I was around nine years old, he and my mother started having problems. I told him I already knew this; that was why he used his first Banked Day to go to the fair, back in 1969. He said I only knew part of the story.

While he was moping around feeling sorry for himself, he

considered using the day to go back to fix his relationship with Cindy. He knew that could mean he may end up not marrying my mother, and he didn't know what that might mean to me, but he was depressed and couldn't think of anything else to do. Every time he and my mother would get into an argument, he would wonder if he and Cindy would have had that fight. So one day he decided he would do it, he would use the Banked Day to go back to Cindy. Dad went to the small room in the bank and said the old Indian phrase for the first time to withdraw a Banked Day. Before he knew it, he was eighteen again.

First, Dad just enjoyed the feeling of being young and carefree. Walking down the street, he saw one of his old buddies who had moved away after high school. After a quick talk, Dad decided he had better do what he came there to do: win back Cindy. He had already determined why she had broken up with him. He knew he had been too jealous and controlling, especially for a young seventeen-year-old girl like Cindy. Now he had to show Cindy how deeply he cared for her, and that he wasn't the jealous type. It's always harder to disprove something isn't the case than to prove it is, but he had a two-part plan.

He walked directly over to Cindy's house. He knew they would have a fight later in the evening, and that's when she would break up with him. Previously, they had gone to a party together, and he got into a fight with another boy who was just talking with her. That would be the last straw for Cindy and the end of their relationship.

This time when Dad knocked on her door, he told her he

needed to spend the evening with his parents. He gave her a hug and told Cindy he trusted her, and that she should go to the party anyway with her girlfriends and have a good time; this was part one. She almost melted in his arms. This was the unselfish side of him she had not seen in a while. Before he left, they agreed to meet in the morning for breakfast at the diner; part two. That is when he would tell Cindy how much she meant to him.

My father went home and had a wonderful time with his parents. It was unusual for him to spend the evening at home, so his parents took advantage of the time by sitting around the table after dinner, just talking. Dad was pleased to see his parents were willing to break out of their normal routine to enjoy the opportunity. Those types of evenings were few and far between. He didn't want the evening to end, so he suggested they all go out for ice cream to cap off the night. His parents loved the idea and they all piled into his father's car for the quick trip downtown to the ice cream shop.

Their conversation didn't lag while they enjoyed their treats. They were oblivious to the time, but it was getting late and the shop was about to close. His parents had already finished their ice cream cones, but since Dad had been doing most of the talking, he still had a bit of his banana-split left. Dad could tell his father was getting tired and knew he had an early start at the bank the next day. So to give his father a break from driving, my father said he would be their chauffeur and drive them home. His parents got into the back seat holding hands like teenagers, and Dad jumped behind the wheel. He put the remainder of his banana-split in his lap as he started home, taking a bite every now and then and carrying on a conversation with

his parents.

I could tell my father was getting a bit upset while he told me this story, as he would stop to clear his throat and wipe his face, but he carried on...

"The echo of the impact was as loud as the statue's thunder."

While he was paying little attention to his driving, another car ran a stop sign and Dad T-boned it, sending the other car off the road and into a tree. Dad and his parents were only slightly hurt, but it didn't look likely that those in the other car would be so lucky. G-Pa-Frank was first to arrive at the other car. Stopping them before they reached the smashed car, he told my father and grandmother to go back to his car and stay there. He would run to get help. My grandfather sprinted down the road to the nearest house and soon returned. He wouldn't let them go to the other car until the ambulance arrived. When they took the limp body from the wrecked car, Dad saw it was Cindy.

When Dad got to that part of the story, he cleared his throat again and just said, "Cindy died on impact and felt no pain."

She was alone in the car, on her way to his house to say how much his trust meant to her. That's what Cindy's girlfriends told him when they called his parents' house to make sure he was okay. As it turned out, the boy Dad fought with before did indeed make advances on Cindy. That only made her think of Dad's trust, and she wanted to be with him.

When my father heard that, he pulled my grandfather aside and told him he was living a Banked Day, and asked how he could re-Bank the day to have a chance to change things. G-Pa-Frank

sadly reminded him that he could not bank days within a year of each other; there was no way to bank the same day twice. Nothing they could do would change what had happened.

The remainder of the day was intensely sad as Dad met with Cindy's parents. He counted the minutes until he would return to the future, eager to leave such a horrible day, but dreading his return since that would seal Cindy's fate.

When Dad returned to his future life, he didn't know what would await him as he left the small room. He didn't have time to let his mind digest what had happened and to remember the years since that day. He ran back to what he hoped would still be his home. He entered the kitchen to find my mother preparing dinner, and held his breath to see if she would welcome him home or accuse him of breaking into her house. She turned, smiled, and asked why he was home early. Dad made up an excuse and went to the bathroom. He sat down and remembered what had happened in the years after Cindy's death. While he sat there and his memory returned, it seemed nothing had really changed in his life. He had still met and married my mother, and they had a son whom he could hear playing in the next room. His memory also told him Cindy had indeed died that night. Instead of going back to make her fall in love with him, the events had killed her.

When Dad returned to work the next day, he looked up at the clock. Both hands had advanced; he could never go back to that day again. He vowed to create a new rule so future generations would not have to suffer such a loss. The new rule: Never use a Banked Day to make someone fall in love with you.

My father then looked at me with moist eyes and said he was afraid when he returned from his second Banked Day, the day at the fair when I was ten years old. He had decided to use that Banked Day a few years later to spice up their lives a bit with some fun. However, when he returned to future-time, he was afraid he had gone back and made my mother fall in love with him. If so, who knew what horrible things may have happened, and who may have been hurt; but everything was alright, actually it was better than ever. The key was my mother was already in love with my father when the day was relived, while Cindy was not.

Dad wiped his eyes and simply said, "using a Banked Day to selfishly bring love to yourself is just too dangerous to all those involved. Just don't do it Bobby!" The tone of his voice startled me. I could tell it had been emotional for him to tell me this story, and I have heeded his advice the best I could; although once, I came dangerously close to violating the same rule.

We both sat there for a few minutes, digesting what had just been said. I gave my father a hug and told him, "Dad, I don't think any less of you… thank you for telling me the truth."

"Bobby, I've been carrying that story with me for a long time. There wasn't anyone I could tell, except my own father, but he didn't want to talk about it. I think he felt guilty for letting me drive that night, which is crazy, but I guess we both felt we needed to be punished for what happened, and since we were the only ones who knew, we punished ourselves. It really helps to be able to tell you the truth, even though I feel ashamed."

"Dad, you only went there looking for love. Don't keep

beating yourself up for that."

"I can't tell you the pain and guilt I've carried with me over Cindy's death… but to make matters worse, I feel ashamed for how I turned my back on you and your mother. Although she never knew about it, I've been trying to make it up to her ever since… but Bobby, what would have happened to you if I had never married your mother? "

Well that is something I hadn't thought about. I sat back as I considered the most obvious result, I wouldn't be alive. I knew that was what my father was also thinking, and I could only imagine how that must make him feel. Finally I managed to say, "Dad, this crazy gift can make you dizzy. What if this and what if that… the combination of possible events is endless… but the fact is, you and Mom did marry… you did have me… and here we are, right here and right now. There's nothing we can do now but to live our lives as they are… taking advantage of each and every day… and honestly… today and this trip are going to be great. I can't think of anyone I'd rather be with right now than you. I love you Dad."

Dad wiped his eyes, looked down for a moment, and then turned his head toward me, "Thanks son. Look who's the mature one now. I love you too Bobby."

We sat there a while longer and then my father smiled and said "Hey Buddy, if we're going to make Hamburg by tonight, we better hit the road."

We returned to the car and continued our journey, leaving the story about Cindy and that Banked Day in the parking lot of the roadside park. I think that conversation helped my father. Maybe he

found some peace, knowing it might help me avoid a similar fate.

We arrived in Hamburg around five o'clock that evening and checked into the first motel we saw. It was nothing special, but it was comfortable and clean. We enjoyed a meal at a local diner and went to bed soon after, eager to get an early start exploring Hamburg the next morning.

VI. Timmah: Protector of Time

After eating breakfast, we started our day at the Hamburg courthouse. We met Mr. Tom Woodman, an interesting man to say the least. He was the county historian who had lived in Hamburg his entire life. With little coaxing, he offered to tell us the "official" history of the town.

Taking a deep breath as if he were about to submerge for a deep-water dive, Mr. Woodman began his story. "Hamburg was formed in 1848, by German immigrants who named the town after the famous city in Germany. The first two public buildings were built in 1851: the jail and the courthouse where we are standing now. Hamburg was incorporated in 1854, and enjoyed slow but steady growth over the next seven years. During the Civil War, many residents joined the Confederate Army under the command of Hamburg's lawyer Van H. Manning. The war never came to Hamburg, but Union troops did occupy it briefly during the Reconstruction."

As Mr. Woodman took his first breath, I realized the Reconstruction period was just after the time when Levi came to town in 1865.

Mr. Woodman gave a sideways glance to make sure we were paying attention, took another deep breath, and continued his monologue. "At the time, Hamburg had close to two hundred residents and was growing rapidly as the trading center of the area. It had a railroad stop and high expectations of becoming the major city in the area. While today it is still considered the seat of Ashley County, Hamburg didn't see the expected growth because the town's proposed new lumber company was built twelve miles away, in what would become the town of Crossett. In the early 1900's, most people in the area were farmers, but thanks to local forests, lumber production became more and more dominant.

He couldn't help it, Mr. Woodman ran out of air. I think he felt a bit defeated that he required a third breath to finish, but he continued with a sense of determination. "After the Depression, many farmers left their farms and went to work in the saw mills or paper mills nearby. Besides the jail and courthouse, the oldest standing structure in town is the Ashley County Museum, which used to be the Watson House... built in 1883..." Mr. Woodman concluded his speech by proudly telling us, "...and since 1970, the gazebo in the town square has been the venue for the Armadillo Festival, held the first weekend in May." Mr. Woodman tried to conceal his gasp for air, as he actually gave a short bow at the end of his performance.

What Mr. Woodman didn't tell us, because no one knew it at the time, was Hamburg's most famous resident would be the future NBA star Scottie Pippin, who played for the Chicago Bulls in the 1990s. However, Scottie was only in Jr. High during our visit to

Hamburg that day.

I can only assume Mr. Woodman had told that story many times, but his enthusiasm was not lost in the retelling. After we listened to Mr. Woodman's standard history lesson, we asked him for the more obscure town history. We posed our questions as research for a summer project I was doing to help with college acceptance. We asked Mr. Woodman if there had been any cultural influence in Hamburg from the American Indians.

Mr. Woodman said, "Well, not really, even though the Choctaw tribe did occupy land near the Arkansas River at one time." We were about to ask our next question when Mr. Woodman added, "There was one prominent Hamburg citizen who was a Choctaw. She was known simply by the name of Timmah... in fact, there's a plaque mentioning her down at the old Watson House, now the county museum."

Dad coyly asked, "Mr. Woodman, could you please tell us more about this Timmah?"

"Well, she had owned a sizable piece of property just outside the city limits, which was sold to the city upon her death back in the 1860's, just after the war ended."

Dad and I gave each other a sideways glance, barely able to conceal our excitement. Dad asked before he really had his thoughts straight, "I know it's been a long time Mr. Woodman, but was there... I mean... well... is anything left of her estate now?"

Mr. Woodman smiled; I think he really liked to share a good story. "The county museum is located next to the town's cemetery, and the oldest part of the cemetery was Timmah's family

burial grounds."

I blurted out in my excitement, "Can we see it?"

Mr. Woodman was a bit surprised by my interest in the cemetery, but informed me with an official tone, "Timmah's section of the cemetery is considered a protected Indian burial ground and is not open to the public, son."

Dad decided now was the time to play our trump card. After looking around the small foyer to the office to ensure our privacy, Dad said, "Mr. Woodman, there is something we haven't told you yet. Our last name is Greenfield, and Levi Greenfield is our ancestor. Since you are knowledgeable on Hamburg's history, I think you may be familiar with that name."

Mr. Woodman physically took a step backward in his surprise. However, he quickly regained his composure and asked in his controlled excitement, "Sir, I do not doubt your claim, but may I see some identification please?"

"Absolutely" my father said as he pulled out his driver's license.

"Oh my word, I can't believe it. Please Sir, would you and your son please step into my office?" As we walked down the short hallway, we could hear Mr. Woodman mumbling in his excitement.

After shutting the door, he shook our hands again and was so excited I thought he might have a heart attack. Also concerned, my father asked him if he was alright. Mr. Woodman assured us his heart was better than new since his surgery; but the question did seem to calm him down a bit, enough anyway that we could now understand him. He asked us questions about what happened to

Levi, and we told him the truth, minus the obvious details. He told us we needed to go to the museum right away. He would call ahead to let the curator know our story, so she would be ready to give us the grand tour. Mr. Woodman said to just ask for Pam. As we were leaving the building, we could hear him on the phone with Pam. He was so excited he could barely get the words out regarding who was on their way to visit her. Just before he hung up, we could hear him confirming plans to play cards with her on Saturday night. It seems there is great cooperation between the courthouse and the county museum, both during and after hours.

Using Mr. Woodman's directions, we quickly drove to the county museum. We had barely parked our car in the museum's parking lot, when Pam came out to greet us.

"Hello Mr. Greenfield, and to you too young Mr. Greenfield" Pam said in a rushed, excited voice. "My name is Pam, and Mr. Woodman has filled me in on your quest for information. Please know I will help you in any way I can."

"Thank you Pam" my father said as he tried to regain his hand from her enthusiastic greeting. "We are most interested to learn all we can about the Indian woman who once lived on this land."

"Well then, we can start right here" Pam said as she pointed to the plaque on a pole about halfway along the walk to the old Watson House, now the museum. Near the bottom of the plaque, it mentioned the land had once been owned by a Choctaw Indian woman named Timmah, which means "Protector of Time." Little did Pam, or anyone in Hamburg, know the significance of Timmah's

name. Before we moved along to enter the Watson House, Pam looked around to ensure we were not overheard and told us one of Hamburg's oldest secrets, while trying to catch her breath from the excitement. "Everyone says the Watson House was built in the 1880's... but the truth is... this was Timmah's actual house... and it was really built twenty years prior... in the early 1860's."

I'm sure Pam could see our confusion mixed with excitement, as she continued telling her secret, now more calmly. "When it was decided to make this the county museum, people thought it would be bad for business if anyone knew an Indian had once lived in the house. So history was rewritten. Then the lie took on a life of its own. It would be too embarrassing if the secret came out now." Pam quickly looked me in the eye and said, "Please don't include that part in your project. I just thought you would like to know since your ancestor Levi had actually owned the house at one time."

"No problem ma'am, I can keep a secret" I said with a sideways glance to my father.

With relief, Pam went on to tell us most of Timmah's original fixtures and furniture were still in the house. Now my father and I were really excited. What clues would we be able to find in this old house?

The structure was only about 800 square feet of interior space, but it had a wonderful wrap-around porch. The house had five rooms: the front parlor, the kitchen, one bedroom, a store room of some kind, and a bathroom. Our tour really started in the kitchen, which was small but very useable, and had a backdoor that led to the

porch. We imagined Timmah cooking the stew for Levi on the old stove standing just feet from us now. We poked our head into the bathroom and noticed the claw-foot tub where Levi fell asleep. Pam made a point of saying how modern the house was back then. It was unusual for the bathroom to be inside the main house in the 1860's. The store room was near the kitchen and we imagined that is where Levi probably slept. It now contained display cases of old photos and artifacts from the early days of Hamburg and the surrounding areas, but nothing about Levi. We walked back toward the front door and stopped in the front parlor. There was a fireplace, the front window looking out onto the porch, a rocking chair and a small table in the corner of the room.

Dad asked Pam if she would mind giving us a moment alone to look around; she was more than obliging. Once Pam left the house, Dad and I actually started giggling.

"Dad, can you believe this?" I said holding my head in my hands so it wouldn't explode.

"Bobby, I can't stop shaking. This place is exactly how I've imagined it for all these years. I can almost see Levi and Timmah in each room."

We went back through all the rooms and spoke aloud how the items matched our family's story about Levi and the old Indian woman who now had a name. Thanks to the care my father and all the G-Pas before him had taken to preserve the details of our family's story, it had stayed amazingly accurate over the generations. We scoured the display cases in the store room for more clues, but didn't find anything pertaining to Levi. We went

back to the front parlor and just looked around, imagining scenes from our family's legend. I was standing at the front window and put my hand on the small table in the corner of the room. I quickly looked down and then over to my father. When he looked at me, all I could do was point at the table. I covered my mouth to keep from screaming and finally whispered, "Dad, this table has four marks on it. Is this the table Timmah used for the statue?"

Dad looked down; there was an oval rug on the hardwood floor. After he checked the door, he came back and lifted the edge of the rug. In the center of the room were four faint marks on the floor. They looked as if they had been burned into the wood. Glancing back to the table, the marks on the floor were an exact match to the dimensions of the table's legs. Dad stood in the middle of the markings on the floor and said, "Bobby, the Life Pole has to be 300 feet from right here."

Looking out the window again, I strained to look right and left, but saw no pole. To my embarrassment, I noticed Pam was in the parking lot looking at me through the window. "Dad, maybe we should leave soon. Pam probably thinks I'm crazy by the look she just gave me."

We put the rug back and exited through the front door. Pam was waiting for us by our car. "Tom, I mean Mr. Woodman, told me you were also interested in seeing the Indian Burial grounds."

"Yes ma'am, if that's alright. I think Bobby here would find it very helpful for his project."

"Well, normally we don't allow that, but considering the circumstances..." She took a quick look around to see if anyone was

nearby, "...I think we can arrange something." Noticing I was about to jump out of my skin, she motioned for me to calm down and said, "But it would have to be after dark, so no one would see us."

"Yes ma'am, I completely understand..." Dad said. "...what time would you like us to come back?"

"I think nine o'clock tonight would be fine. The museum will be closed and no one should be around at that hour. Come on back then, and we will take a little look around." Pam seemed pleased with herself.

We agreed on the arrangements and slowly drove away from Timmah's house. We went back to town, picked up burgers, and found the city park where we could eat and talk in privacy. We finished our meal while we discussed everything we had discovered at Timmah's house. The rest of the afternoon and early evening was spent driving around Hamburg, soaking in all we could. While the day seemed to drag on forever, it finally came time to go back to the museum.

When we returned to the parking lot, Pam and Mr. Woodman were there to greet us. Pam said, "I hope you don't mind, but I asked Mr. Woodman to join us, since it is nighttime."

"No. Of course not, in fact, the more the merrier." Dad said. It made perfect sense for Pam to want someone else there, and we could tell they were both very excited to take us inside Timmah's family burial grounds.

There was a tall wrought iron fence around Timmah's burial grounds to keep it secure. Pam unlocked the gate and we entered using four flashlights to light our way. The private grounds were not

very large compared to the size of the town's cemetery, adjacent to where we now were. Our eyes immediately focused on a marble tombstone on the far side of several mounds. Those mounds had long since lost any markers, but they were obviously where Timmah's family members were buried. When we reached the marble tombstone, we were able to see the bold and simple inscription; it read:

Timmah – Protector of Time

1821 – 1865

"Dad, she was only forty-four."

I had always assumed the old Indian woman would have been older than forty-four years old. Dad quietly told me, "Bobby, back in those days, each year was hard on the body and medicine was not as advanced as it is now. So a lifespan of forty-four years in the mid-1800s was indeed long."

We noticed a small hill around the corner of several large cottonwood trees, still within the fence. With our flashlight to guide us, we made our way up the hill and there it was: the Life Pole. Pam said it was amazing the wood had lasted all these years, but it seemed to have been petrified by an unknown type of element. Dad and I immediately knew it was the effect of the electricity from the lightning that transformed the wood. We spent the next twenty minutes studying the pole. We found the figure that was repeated in each of the sections, indicating someone had visited multiple generations. The top of the pole was flat, and we imagined how the counterpart to the statue would have looked up there. We smiled

knowing it was now on top of our clock back in O'Fallon. There was one more interesting part on the pole. Toward the top were two boxes carved into the wood. The left box was empty and smooth. The right box had many marks in it. We couldn't count them from where we stood, but we guessed there were around twenty-five. Later that night we concluded those boxes may have been where banked and used days were tracked. If we were correct, the twenty-five or so marks indicated approximately eight generations of Timmah's family had used the power of the statue. In those days, a generation typically occurred every fifteen to twenty years. If we were correct, the statue had been in Timmah's family for approximately 150 years. We could only wonder if the statue started with her family, or if it had been passed to them, as Timmah had passed it to Levi.

We realized Tom and Pam were growing a bit tired of us looking at the Life Pole, so we said we were ready to leave. Tom spoke non-stop all the way back to the car. He was so excited he was repeating what he had already told us, but we were just glad he and Pam had gone out of their way to show us Timmah's burial grounds.

Pam asked "Well Mr. Bobby, will you please send me a copy of your report when you finish it? I'd love to see your perspective on what Tom and I spend so much of our lives devoted to."

"Absolutely ma'am... I'll be sure to send you a copy. Thanks for all your help today." I didn't feel good about lying to Pam, but I knew I could never tell her the truth about our trip.

My father shook hands with Mr. Woodman and thanked him

and Pam for all their help and information they had provided us. As we drove away from the museum, I looked back to see Pam getting into Mr. Woodman's car. I guessed they were getting an early start to their card game.

We spent the night back at the motel. Before we turned out the lights, I said, "Dad, I had hoped to find just one clue on this trip, and, well, we hit the jackpot!"

"Bobby, this trip filled in so many missing parts to the story. I can't wait to tell your G-Pas what we found out today. I suspect the more we think about this trip, more and more new questions will come to us. I doubt this is the last time we will be in Hamburg... but for now, let's get some rest."

I know I didn't sleep that night, and I suspected neither did Dad. We got up early the next day and drove straight through the next night to get home in time to rest before graduation. While it had been an adventure, the trip had been draining. The adrenaline of the discovery kept us going for the drive, but we immediately fell into our beds when we got home. The trip had been a huge success. I knew then it would alter the details of what future generations would hear on their sixteenth birthday.

VII.   Dangers with a Safety Net

I was home for summer break in 1977, after completing my first year at college. I had learned just enough to realize how much I didn't know, about my academics and life in general. Most of my college buddies had no idea what they wanted to do after graduation. In some ways I envied the freedom that brought them, but it gave me comfort and confidence to already know what my future career would be. I was part of a banking family and, with Timmah's gift, I knew where I would spend my life.

It was the third Sunday of the month, which meant all the Greenfields would be at my parents' house for dinner. While my mother and grandmother were in the kitchen preparing the feast, G-Pa-Frank said he had good news for just "us guys."

"Okay everyone; clear your calendars for the weekend of June 12th. The four of us are going on a fishing trip. Mr. Hathorn is letting us borrow his house over on Crooked Lake for the weekend."

My father, probably the best fisherman in the family, jumped on the invitation. "You know I'll be there. So how did you swing that deal?"

"Oh, Mr. Hathorn has been a great client of ours for decades.

He was in my office last week to review his portfolio, and then we started talking about his retirement. He and his wife are going to Colorado in June to visit their daughter and her family. I mentioned how I'm still a few years away from retirement, and he suggested I should take advantage of their lake house while they are gone; the fish should really be biting then. So we figured out the logistics and we are set to go."

I was glad all four Greenfield generations would have an opportunity to be together to discuss Timmah's gift. During my year at college, I didn't have many chances to take family walks and talk about my thoughts and questions. So I often found myself sitting in my dorm room thinking about Hamburg and all we learned there, as well as my father's stories from the trip. Naturally I thought about how and when I might bank my first day, and what I would do with it. Little did I know it would be several years before I would finally move the hands on the old clock.

The big day arrived and we all met at G-Pa-Raymond's house, where we loaded his Suburban and hit the road. Judging by the amount of gear we were taking, we were ready to cross the country for a few weeks; but our weekend trip to Crooked Lake was only eight miles from O'Fallon, near the town of Caseyville.

The drive to the lake took just a few minutes, but finding Mr. Hathorn's cabin was a bit more difficult. We eventually found the practically hidden dirt driveway that wound its way toward the lake. The cabin looked a bit rough from the outside, but once we were through the front door we realized it had been remodeled with all the modern conveniences of the late-1970s.

After we laid claim to our bedrooms and unloaded our gear, which took a while, we walked down to the shed near the shore of the lake. There we found Mr. Hathorn's fishing boat, which was really a row-boat with a trolling motor. G-Pa-Raymond and G-Pa-Frank didn't take long to offer the boat to my father and me. They said they preferred to fish off the bank, but we knew they were a bit leery of getting in the small boat. That was fine with us and we soon settled into our positions. Those on the bank found nice shade trees to set up shop, while Dad and I put the boat in the water.

Crooked Lake was really a man-made reservoir that resembled a wide river in shape. The lake is stocked each year by the Forest Service which provides good fishing for Bluegill, Largemouth Bass, and Yellow Perch. After just a few hours of fishing, Dad and I caught plenty of fish for our evening Bar-B-Q. The day's heat was at its max, so we made our way back to the others, who had also caught their limit. After we cleaned our fish, we spent the afternoon sitting on the back porch and tossing horseshoes in the shaded grassy yard between the house and the lake.

As dusk approached, we got our second wind and started preparing for the feast. My G-Pas all offered their advice on how I should stack the charcoal in a proper pyramid to achieve optimum air circulation for even and quick burning. As the briquettes were turning white, we all chipped in to prepare and then take our side dishes out to the picnic table on the back porch. Our family isn't really a beer drinking bunch, but fishing trips are the exception. We took the cooler out to the porch and each enjoyed an ice cold Hamm's beer. G-Pa-Raymond was our chief-chef and took control

of the grill. Once the fish were cooked to his satisfaction, he brought our bounty to the table. The only thing to be heard for the next twenty minutes was the sound of our forks clicking plates. Maybe it was skipping lunch that made everything taste so good, but we enjoyed our meal too much to talk. After cleaning up, we all went back to the porch to relax and spend the evening.

The mosquitoes were now making their meal of us and we were about to retreat inside, when G-Pa-Frank noticed Mr. Hathorn's fire ring near the lake. We quickly made a fire and sat within the smoke barrier it provided that kept the mosquitoes away. I was on my third beer of the evening, and while I wasn't keeping count, I suspect my elders had enjoyed a few more than me. Hey, we weren't going anywhere, and the ambiance of sitting by the fire next to the lake was hypnotizing, so extra beers were certainly fine. Besides, a little buzz from the beer would help drown out the buzz from the cicadas.

Every thirteen years in southern Illinois, the cicadas have their mating season. As with most species, the male is always trying to attract the attention of a potential mate. In the case of the cicada, the male makes a long mating call by contracting membranes within the abdomen. When several thousand cicada males do this together, the resulting noise can rise and fall in waves of pulsating sound. This has a rippling effect that seems to carry on throughout the night without pause. As the cicadas in the trees across the lake serenaded us with their love song, our conversation turned toward Timmah's gift, as it usually does when we are all together, alone.

Since our trip to Hamburg, the four of us had shared many

walks discussing what we learned about Timmah. The new details seemed to fuel our curiosity, and we typically framed our discussions around what if this or that should happen on a Banked Day.

G-Pa-Frank asked me, "So Bobby, now that you have a year of college under your belt, do you have any new what-if questions about our gift?"

Since this was a favorite topic of ours, I knew it would come up so I was prepared. "Well G-Pa-Frank, I was wondering what it would be like if we had the ability to transfer Banked Days."

G-Pa-Frank always did have a low tolerance for alcohol, so he was acting a bit silly. "You mean if you could give me one of your days, so I would have four and you would only have two? Because I'll take one of yours if you don't want it."

"That would be interesting, and I think I'll keep all of mine thanks, but that isn't really what I meant. I was thinking more along the lines where someone had already banked a day, and then another person in our family used it." This was a new twist to our discussions and I could tell it caught everyone's attention when they all leaned back in their chairs to think it over.

Dad was the first to speak up, "I'll start by saying that I don't think the gift works that way... but to play along... maybe it would be like when you have two of your own days banked, and you have to concentrate on which day you wanted to relive when you cash it in. So I think the person who originally banked the day would have to be involved, to somehow give 'permission' to let another person use the day."

Then G-Pa-Frank said, "Well, let's say you could figure out the logistics of how to cash in on someone else's day. I think the really interesting part would be that you would probably take on their appearance once you were in their past. Wouldn't it be strange to see yourself in the mirror as someone else? You know, since everyone would think you were the other person, you could really hurt their reputation, and their future for that matter. So overall I have to say, I'm glad the gift doesn't allow transferring days; it's just too dangerous."

Everyone chimed in and basically agreed with G-Pa-Frank, and congratulated me on a novel scenario. G-Pa-Frank stood up and announced he was going to grab one of my beers since he couldn't have one of my days. We playfully raced to the cooler, where I handed him a beer in a mock-presentation of his trophy.

After we all opened another beer and settled back down in our chairs, Dad offered the next what-if. "Here's something I've been meaning to ask you all for a while. What if you had banked a day just before a huge event in history, and let's say this event was something bad. How would you try to prevent it from happening... or would you even try? One event that comes to mind is Pearl Harbor."

Due to G-Pa-Frank's history with WWII he immediately replied. "Well son, if I woke up on December 8th and I had banked a day two weeks earlier; I honestly don't know what I could have done. I know I would try to do something to save all those people, but who would believe me?"

G-Pa-Raymond said, "If you warned the Navy that Japan was

about to attack Pearl Harbor, they would ignore you. Until December 8th that is, and then you would be in jail for suspicion of treason."

Then I added, "It would be better if your Banked Day was a few months before the attack. Then you could warn the Navy of the weakness in our defenses that allowed the Japanese to sneak up on Pearl Harbor undetected. That way, perhaps changes could be made in time before the attack, without putting yourself in a suspicious position."

"I agree Bobby," replied my father, "but then you have the always present question: how does that affect the future? If we could thwart the attack on Pearl Harbor, there would be a huge shift on who lived and died that day. You also have to think about how the war itself would play out. Would the atomic bombs still be used on Hiroshima and Nagasaki? Even if dropping those bombs were delayed just a bit, many more troops on both sides would be killed in action each day… which then affects future generations."

I sipped on my beer thinking about my father's comments, and then responded. "It would seem reasonable that as long you acted quickly, it might be okay. If the time between Dec 7th and when you used the Banked Day was kept short, there wouldn't be much time for history to go too far down one path before it was changed. That would minimize the potential damage from any erased history… but like you said… a lot can happen in just a few days. The longer you wait, the more history would be changed."

The smoke from the fire was running thin and the mosquitoes were finding their way to us again. As I jumped up to put more

wood on the fire, it made me wonder if we made the right decision to stay outside for our talk. That inspired me for my next what-if.

"Alright, I have another one for you guys. In a few years, I will graduate from college and will face a decision that everyone has at that time. What job offer should I accept and where should I live?" No one said a word, but I could see the tension on everyone's face by the fire-light. It was just assumed I would work at our bank after college. I put everyone at ease by saying, "Now for me, that is an easy decision..." Without looking, I could hear bodies shifting and a slow exhale could be felt around the fire. "...but for my fellow classmates, that is a very big decision. So what if you used Banked Days as a safety net for life's big decisions? If you found out later that you made the wrong choice, you could relive that Banked Day and take the other path. So for example, if I had decided to go away to work somewhere and then found out that it was a mistake, I could go back, change my original choice, and start working at our bank."

My father jumped on that like the fish on our hooks earlier in the day. "Bobby, I think what you were saying about Pearl Harbor applies here too. The longer you wait, the more likely there will be big differences between your original and revised history. Those differences don't just affect you... they also affect everyone touched by the ripple effect."

While my father was talking, I noticed G-Pa-Raymond seemed to become a bit anxious. He got up to get another beer while G-Pa-Frank said, "I agree. Most big decisions in life take a long time to determine if they were right or wrong. That amount of time

takes you way down one path in history, and to completely erase everything that happened on that path could have huge consequences."

By now G-Pa-Raymond was back in his chair and seemed upset. My father noticed this too and asked if he was alright.

G-Pa-Raymond lifted his hand as if to say he was fine, but he couldn't speak for a while. We all sat there quietly, letting the cicadas fill the silence as he gathered himself. When he seemed composed, he said, "You all are absolutely right about the relationship between time and the distance you take down a path in history. What's hard to know is if the potential outcome is worth the risk. You just can't know for sure... but still... you may have to make a choice... I did."

In an instant, we shifted gears from a light-hearted what-if discussion to what we knew would be something intense. None of us said a word. We just waited until G-Pa-Raymond was ready to tell us what happened. He quickly finished his beer and began.

"After I finished college, Peggy and I were married in the old town church. Both our families were there, and it was a big event in O'Fallon since Dad was the town banker. After the wedding, we lived with my parents while we decided where we wanted to live. Peggy liked the idea of living in town, and I thought I might prefer to be on some acreage... something a bit more remote. Then one day, Peggy came to me all depressed and told me she was tired of O'Fallon and wanted to move away. She wanted to move to California. I'm not sure why she picked California... I think it just sounded far away. That was a shock to me and I felt torn between

my new wife and my home. Home to me had always been about family, and when you consider our gift is also here, I had never considered leaving O'Fallon... but she persisted and eventually I agreed to leave. I wasn't sure that was the right thing to do, but I had to make a decision. It was very difficult to tell my parents, and you can only imagine the conversation I had with my father. After all, he had been the one to receive the gift directly from Timmah, and he had hoped it would carry on through many Greenfield generations... but I had promised Peggy we would leave and I couldn't break my word to her. At my father's suggestion, I banked a day before we left. It was exactly what you said, it was a safety net. He said I could always come back and start over again in O'Fallon if things didn't work out for us in California. So I banked the day and we soon said our goodbyes... we moved to California."

G-Pa-Raymond stopped and looked at us, waiting for one of us to say something. After a long silence, his son said, "Dad, why haven't you told us about this before?"

"Frank, that's a fair question, but let me continue and I think you will understand." G-Pa-Raymond tried to take a sip from his beer can, and dropped it at his feet when he realized it was empty. With only a slight hesitation he continued, "We moved to a small town called Morgan Hill, in southern California. The land there is fertile and they grew grapes and garlic in the hills outside of town. Anyway, with my background I got a job at a local bank, and we settled down in a small house nearby."

I'm not sure what the others were thinking, but I was completely confused. How could he have moved to California?

And if he moved there, how could we all be sitting here together now?

"After a few months, Peggy became pregnant. We didn't really plan it, but those things just happen sometimes." He tried a faint smile, but the tension was too great for it to have any effect on us.

G-Pa-Frank asked, "Dad, was I born in California then?"

His father didn't answer; instead he stared into the fire and continued. "The baby was a little girl... and she was still-born."

G-Pa-Frank jolted to his feet and practically screamed, "I had a sister? How could you keep that from me?" He slumped back into his seat as quickly as he stood, leaving us to worry he had fainted. He was alright, just very upset.

G-Pa-Raymond leaned forward in his chair and took his son's hand. "Frank, this secret has been eating at me for decades, but please let me continue and finish my story before I lose my nerve." His son, well all of us really, stared at him wondering what else he could possibly have left to tell us.

"Peggy was deeply depressed after this. I missed so much time from the bank to take care of her... they had no choice but to let me go. With no income, we decided we should come back to O'Fallon. Plus it would be good for her to be around friends and family. After we had been home for several weeks, my father reminded me about my Banked Day. I struggled with the decision, but Peggy was only getting worse... I felt I had to do something, anything. So I went to the bank and cashed in my day."

My father asked, "G-Pa-Raymond, did your father talk with

you about what to expect when you returned? Those were the early days of using the gift… how well did you understand what could happen."

"Joe, when I look back on our conversation, I think he was more interested in having us back to stay and for us to grow our family in O'Fallon, than any consequences that may happen in California. So no, we didn't really discuss what might happen after I relived my Banked Day."

G-Pa-Raymond jumped back into his story before he could be interrupted again, intent to finish telling his secret. "When I went back to that day, I told Peggy we needed to stay in O'Fallon. I tried to position it as her parents would need her as they grew older. She saw through that and we had a huge fight. While we ended up staying in O'Fallon, I don't think she ever really forgave me for breaking my word. It took a few years, but eventually she became pregnant again… she had no clue she had been pregnant before. I was excited but scared to death something would happen to the baby again. So toward the end of the pregnancy, I paid for a doctor from St. Louis to stay with us. I wanted to take every precaution I could to ensure a better outcome… but as we all know, Peggy died while giving birth to Frank... the rest of our history in O'Fallon is exactly what you all know to be true."

After a few moments, G-Pa-Frank slowly looked at his father and said, "Dad, if you had stayed in California, Mom would be alive today."

"No Frank! Never consider that as a possibility. She may have become pregnant again and the outcome could have been the

same, or worse. The doctor said I could have lost you too if he had not been there. There were complications with the umbilical cord and you nearly died. If that had happened, I don't know what I would have done. Frank, the only thing that gave me the strength to move forward with my life, was having you."

As the news settled in for all of us, G-Pa-Raymond continued. "After Peggy died, I did have talks with my father about what may have changed due to my actions. We couldn't know what may have been undone in California, but it helped knowing Frank would carry on the Greenfield bloodline. It's a shame Dad died before his grandson, Joe, was born... but I think he died happy knowing he was leaving a legacy."

We all stared into the dying fire for a while, thankful for the cicadas to lessen the silence. After the last flicker of the flame seemed to disappear, G-Pa-Frank swatted a mosquito on his forehead and said, "Well gents, it looks like our fire has run its course. I don't know about the rest of you, but I think I'm ready for bed."

We all were looking for a way to gracefully retreat to our rooms to digest the evening's events, so we agreed to call it a night. We doused the ashes with water and returned to the house. As I was closing the door to my room, I saw G-Pa-Raymond in the bathroom, brushing his teeth. I made my way over to him and said, "G-Pa, I'm sorry you were put in a position where you had to make an impossible choice. Just know that your great-grandson is thankful you decided to come back to O'Fallon."

Those few words seemed to melt away years of guilt and regret. So much tension was released from his shoulders, he looked

noticeably taller. He gave me a strong hug and said, "Bobby, when I look at you, your father, and his father, I know I did the right thing… but I have always had to bare the guilt that my decision may have killed my wife. I'll never really know, but your kind words are music to my old ears."

The next morning, we agreed to forgo any more fishing and just head for home. First, we took time to make sure the house was cleaner than we found it, and then we drove the short distance to O'Fallon.

There have been many what-if discussions on our walks since that weekend, but the night of our fishing trip was the last for G-Pa-Raymond. He said he was getting too old to take our walks, but we knew he no longer wanted to be involved with such discussions. While I was just beginning my adventure with Timmah's gift, it seemed G-Pa-Raymond's interest in banking days died with the fire that night.

VIII. Banking My First Day

It was the summer of 1979. I was between my junior and senior year at the state college; my life was going really well. I didn't have any true responsibilities, and I had a great group of friends. Plus, I had just met the girl who would become my wife, Carrie. My only other real relationship had started in high school and ended in my second year at college. Her name was Judith, and like most first-loves, I thought it would last forever but I hadn't learned the lesson from the mistake my father had made with Cindy. I had been too jealous and eventually drove her away, but my broken heart was mended the first time I saw Carrie. Carrie was medium height with an attractive build, but her beautiful, large eyes were her most dramatic feature. Sometimes it seemed those eyes could see into my soul.

My days that summer were filled with rehearsing with my band and hanging out at the swimming hole, created when the quarry flooded. The music on the radio was better than we realized at the time; good enough to now be considered Classic Rock. The Eagles were my favorite band and they seemed to dominate the radio airways, which was fine by me. Our band tried to cover their songs

but we weren't very successful. We enjoyed playing together and our friends were kind enough to say we were good. However, we knew better than to think we could ever go professional. It was just for fun, in a very fun time of my life.

It was mid July, and I woke up thinking about when I was ten years old, when my family and friends went to the fair. It was hard to believe it was twelve years ago, almost to the day. I sat up in my bed as if a bolt of lightning had just run through me. Maybe it had. Today would be like many days I already had that summer, and many more I would have before I went back to school in the fall. Next summer would be very different. I would have graduated and may even have a job already. This was the best summer of my youth, and I knew it. I figured one day I would want to relive a day during this summer, and today was the perfect day to bank.

First, I had some planning to do. How would I explain my absence to my parents? I decided I would tell them I was going camping with my friends. Then I thought I'd better tell my friends something, because what if my parents called them or their parents to confirm my story? This could quickly get messy. I finally decided to tell my parents I was going camping with Jimmy. I asked Jimmy to tell his Aunt Gertrude, whom he lived with, that we were going camping to cover the story with my parents. Thinking it through, I realized that meant Jimmy had to stay away from home that night to cover the story with his aunt. To make it work, Jimmy actually had to go camping alone; so naturally when I asked him for my favor, he wanted to know what I was up to. I said I needed an alibi in case Carrie and I hit it off and wanted some privacy, even

though I knew I didn't want to move too fast with Carrie. I really liked her and didn't want to rush anything. Jimmy was definitely a child of the 60's and I knew his reply would be "groovy man, it's cool." So the plan was set.

I went down to the bank soon after it opened. My father was busy with a client and the tellers thought nothing of me stepping into the back offices. Once I knew I was alone, I headed down the long narrow hallway my father had taken me years ago. I knew the door to the small room would be locked and hoped the key was hidden in the same place my father had previously recovered it on my sixteenth birthday. It was.

I closed the door to the room and stared at the odd little statue sitting on the table. It looked exactly as it did years ago. I mentally ran through the old Indian saying my father had taught me, which I had practiced a million times during the last few years. I made sure the table was sitting on its marks, and likewise the statue matched the marks on the table. Just as my father had instructed me, I put my hand on the statue, gave a quick thanks to Timmah, closed my eyes and recited Timmah's saying.

That was the last thing I remembered until I woke up the next day. I was lying on the floor of the small room. Strangely, I had a blanket covering me and my head was on a pillow. I was quite comfortable, but couldn't figure out what happened. I sat there for a while, reconstructing the events of the withdrawal of my Banked Day. My last memory was saying the ancient words, and then nothing. I guessed that was normal since I had just banked a day and it would be empty until used in the future. It felt odd knowing I had

skipped a day that everyone else had lived. I wondered what Jimmy and Rob had done during my missing day. How was Jimmy's camping trip? What world news had occurred? Not that I ever watched or was interested in world news back then, but it still crossed my mind. An entire world had just lived a day without me. It all seemed very surreal.

Just then the door of the small room opened, it was Dad. He was carrying a bag containing a fast-food breakfast and a plastic container of orange juice. He smiled at me and said, "I thought you might be hungry, so I brought you a little something."

Instinctively I said, "Ah, yea, in fact I'm starving." as I reached for the bag.

"That's normal. In real-time, your body hasn't eaten for a day. Just a suggestion for the next time, you may want to bring a little snack for when you wake up."

My father's instructions made me feel a bit childish, but then I realized only someone who had been through banking a day would know what it feels like when you return. I was lucky to have the benefit of my father's experience with such an unusual process. It must have been very difficult and scary for Levi to face all this on his own. So I stopped feeling silly and realized what a gift I really had.

However, I was still a bit embarrassed that he knew I had banked a day. I was worried he would think I had wasted one of my precious days. After all, we only get three days to bank and he was probably wondering what made this day so special. My fears were quickly put aside when he said, "Hey Bobby, I think you made an

excellent choice picking a day in this season of your life to bank. After all, we are only young once, or so."

I sat up and asked, "How did you know I was here, and I was banking a day? Did you see me sneak through the offices? Oh man, did someone else see me?"

Dad quickly put me at ease and recounted the events of the previous day, as he saw them. He was in his office when a clap of thunder boomed so loudly that pictures rattled on the wall. He ran out to the lobby to check the hands of the old clock. The minute hand had slowly crept back to the 58th mark. He knew right away a new day had been banked. Dad had to play along with the confusion, so he would not look strangely calm to everyone else. He went outside and found all the other businessmen on the block doing the same thing. They were all looking up to the blue, clear sky and wondering what the noise had been. A couple of the older men sitting on the park bench, recounted years past when a similar event had occurred, and how they never did find out what it was. This made Dad almost laugh out loud, but he faked a cough to conceal his chuckle. Once everyone was convinced no damage had occurred to their property, they went back into their respective buildings and resumed business as usual. Dad knew that day was anything but usual, but he played along.

After everyone in the bank settled down from the strange occurrence, Dad found the blanket and pillow in a back office. He sometimes used the bedding when he worked late and just slept at the bank instead of going home. He quickly made his way down the narrow hall and found me lying in a heap on the floor of the hidden

room. I must have fallen from the table when I went unconscious. He made me comfortable with the pillow and blanket and left me there all day and night. Then, twenty-four hours after the thunder clap, Dad brought me breakfast.

Dad asked, "So apart from being hungry, how do you feel? I've always wanted to ask someone just as they returned, to see if my experience is common. When I've asked my elders, they were always sketchy on the details."

"Well, I was definitely hungry. Thanks again for the breakfast... but apart from that, I guess it's a bit like waking up slightly hung-over."

"How do you know what it feels like to be hung-over?"

"Ah, well, that's just an analogy... I'm only guessing how that would feel of course." I doubt he bought it, but he was nice enough to let it go. "But I do feel a bit groggy and confused."

"Wait until you relive a Banked Day. That's when it really takes a while to clear things up, because you have new memories to filter into your reality."

"How long does it take to remember everything from that day, and how it changed the years since?"

"From what I've heard, it varies for everyone... but for me... it starts fuzzy... more or less just a gut-feeling of the Banked Day. It's like recalling a vague memory from when you were little. Remember what it was like when you would hear the song over the speaker of the ice cream truck?"

"You bet. Even now when I hear it, I'm immediately taken back to sitting on our front porch at dusk, feeling the warm breeze of

a summer's evening… anxiously waiting for the truck to come around the corner."

"Exactly… you remember the feeling you had at that time. And often the memory is triggered by one or more of your senses… like hearing that song, or feeling a warm breeze at dusk. That's the same way I start to remember a Banked Day. The first thing I remember is the emotion of the day. Then I'll remember smells, tastes, sounds, things like that. Finally, the details of the day will come to me. As they do, my mind processes what has happened during the years since that day. It's similar to peeling an onion, exposing one layer at a time. The whole process can take several hours, and it can be confusing… for me anyway."

Then Dad asked me when I thought I might use my Banked Day in the future. I considered it for a minute and guessed it would likely be when my daily routine was dramatically different from what it is now. I said, "Someday in the future, my life will probably be more complicated, and I may want to return to when things were simpler."

Dad digested what I had just said, "That may be true, but no matter where we are in the phases of our lives, we always think the grass is greener in a different phase. When we are older, we think how it used to be simpler when we were young. And when we are young, we think things will be better when we are older. What we should realize is each stage of our lives is just different, that's all. Typically, only bad things happen when people either try to rush or hang on to a time in their lives that isn't their current season. It may be fun for a while, but like the 'Indian Summer,' the natural order of

the seasons will eventually prevail. Each brings new and interesting events and circumstances into our lives… it's best if we just embrace the differences. The only real constant that I would like to change, is our bodies get older and you feel the aches a bit more each year."

I sat there and considered what Dad just said. When I was in high school, I thought how much easier things were in elementary school. And I suppose once I'm out of college, these years will seem simple compared to going to work; even though I wish I could start my career and be independent right now. Stopping to consider my own thoughts, I guess I was as guilty as anyone else, wishing my life away. I made a vow to myself to remember my father's advice: each season isn't better, worse, easier or harder than others, they are just different.

Dad brought me back to the conversation when he said, "One of the things I enjoy the most when I use a Banked Day is how young and strong I feel. It's a shame we don't appreciate our health as much as we should. The gift of youth is just wasted on the young." We had a good laugh at his insight, but agreed it was indeed true.

As I sat there finishing my breakfast and regaining my faculties, I asked my father, "When you look back at your life, what phase was the best?"

Dad smiled and said, "Hey, I'm not done yet. I'm not that old you know… actually, I hope the best part of my life is somewhere in my future. Still, I think the time we have shared talking about Timmah's gift has probably been the best, so far anyway."

We spent a bit more time recounting some of the discussions

from our walks, and Dad made sure I felt fine before he would let me start moving around. It didn't take too long for me to recover and we gathered our things to leave.

Before we left the small room, he told me I should go home and get some rest, but I may want to dirty myself up a bit first, since I was supposed to have been camping all night. We walked down the narrow hall and through the lobby, where I glanced at the big clock. It indeed was showing 2:58. My day was officially in the bank. Although I felt excited to finally be in the "game," I was nervous about the heavy responsibility now ahead of me, to use the day safely. It gave me comfort knowing Dad, my G-Pas, and I would have many more opportunities for our walks. I knew there was still much for me to learn before I would feel ready to withdraw my day. Still, there was no doubt I was on a high from the excitement of what I had done that day. I knew my Banked Day would give me great joy sometime in my future. As time would tell, I was right. I only wish the circumstances could have been better.

IX. What a Day it Was, Is...

As my life unfolded, I graduated from college, and I did take a job at our bank. No big surprise there I suppose. I knew I would end up at our bank, but thought I might begin my career somewhere else first. Perhaps I would venture away from O'Fallon for a few years, to see how the rest of the world looked. St. Louis and Chicago weren't very far away in mileage, but hugely different in lifestyle. It's not as if I didn't have my chance. I had an offer to work at a large financial institution just outside Chicago. I mulled it over for almost a month before I declined the offer. The fact was I belonged in O'Fallon, my family and friends were there. I knew my future was there, so I decided to start living my future now and I accepted my father's offer. His plan had me starting at the bottom of the banking hierarchy. My father insisted I learn the business from the ground floor up. We both knew I would run the bank one day, so his arrangement was fine with me. I began as an assistant teller, was quickly promoted to teller, and was gradually working my way to become a personal banker, helping setup loans and mortgages.

One day in the early summer of 1981, while my father was away on business, I was doing my basic duties at my desk when a

very loud clap of thunder rocked my small office. I knew right away what it had to be, but I acted surprised like everyone else. The hands on the clock had settled on 2:57. Another day had been banked. When the commotion settled, I secretly made my way down the narrow hall to the small room. I found Dad lying across the table; sound asleep with his blanket draped over his shoulders and his head on the pillow. I could tell he had done this before, he looked quite comfortable. I noticed an ice chest on the floor containing food and drinks, waiting for his return. I gently straightened his neck and made him as comfortable as I could, then I left the room quietly closing the door. When I turned around, I had the surprise of my life.

There, walking down the hall towards me was my father.

"Dad?"

My hand was still on the doorknob. Not knowing what I should expect, I reopened the door and looked in to see Dad still sitting at the table. After several double glances, I realized he was in both places at once.

Dad saw my confusion, "Bobby, it's okay. Don't be frightened. Tell me; am I still at the table?"

I looked in once again, and there he was. "Yes. I can see you both in the hall and at the table. This is really freaky Dad."

As if talking to himself, Dad said, "I knew it. G-Pa-Raymond once told me this would happen, but I wasn't sure if he was telling me the truth."

He came closer to the door with hesitation in his step. When he was almost to me, I asked, "Do you want to see yourself?"

He frowned at first and then smiled, "Sure, why not?"

He looked in through the doorway and saw himself lying there. He gave me a glance, and then slowly walked into the small room. The instant he crossed the door's threshold and entered the room, the image of my father disappeared from the small table. This startled him so much he stumbled back out of the room. Just then, he reappeared at the table. The next few moments were filled with Dad stepping into and out of the small room, watching himself play an odd game of hide and seek.

Regaining his composure, Dad locked the door, stored the key and told me to follow him; he had great plans for the day.

We entered the lobby, and Dad walked over to Reba, the head teller. He told her how nice she looked and gave her a big hug. Reba looked at him oddly. First, he wasn't supposed to be there that day, and second, why was he acting so affectionate? He had seen her just yesterday when they closed the bank. Dad realized the situation and quickly recovered by telling her that his meetings had been postponed, and he and his son were going to take off the rest of the day.

As Reba was wishing us a good day, we turned toward the lobby and Dad spotted John Miller sitting in the waiting chairs. I took a few steps before I realized Dad wasn't with me, he was in deep thought, still looking at Mr. Miller. I returned to him and asked, "Dad, what's the matter... do you need to speak with Mr. Miller?"

After some hesitation, he said, "No, not with Mr. Miller... but I do need to speak with Stephanie... give me just a minute."

I stayed there while Dad ducked into Stephanie's office.

Stephanie was a senior lending officer, and I could see she was giving my father a strange look as he spoke with her. He wasn't in her office long and when he returned to me, Dad just said, "Okay, we can go now."

As we were leaving the bank, I looked up to notice the clock still read 2:57. I concluded the clock continued to register the day as having been banked but not yet used. My father was in the process of living the Banked Day, so the hands would not move forward until he returned to the future.

We made our way across the street and sat on the same bench where I'm sitting now, recounting my story. The first thing Dad said was, "Sorry about that Bobby, but I had to try to help John out there."

"What do you mean... how did you help him?

"Well, John is applying for a personal loan... so he can buy an engagement ring. When I saw him sitting there, I remembered all the times he came into the bank to make his monthly loan payment."

"So, isn't that a good thing?"

"Not in his case. You see... his new fiancée accepted the ring and then disappeared with it the following week... leaving John alone to make the payments for two years. I don't know if it will help, but I asked Stephanie to delay his loan for a couple of weeks. Maybe that's enough time for his would-be-fiancée to leave town without his ring."

"Wow... well, good for you Dad. Assuming she still leaves, Mr. Miller will be heartbroken, but at least he won't have the financial burden... so, apart from doing good deeds, what else is

new, or old, with you?"

"Well... my big news is I retired from the bank yesterday, in the future of course."

I knew he was back from sometime in the future, but it was interesting to be able to pinpoint Dad's return from such a milestone in his life. I reached over and shook his hand saying, "Congratulations Dad... you certainly worked hard and you deserve it."

"Thanks son. But I'm not here to talk about me... I'm here for you. Bobby, when you started working at the bank, I was so proud of you. I knew then, I wanted to bank a day and come back to relive it once I retired. I always enjoyed being a banker, right up to my last day at work. Still, I knew those days spent teaching you the business would be some of the best of my career. Son, I watched you grow from a young kid just out of college to a man who was ready to take the reins of the bank when I retired. It's been such a pleasure to watch you grow... as a banker... but more importantly as a man. I wanted to come back to this day to praise you, and to encourage you. Your future is so bright... both inside and outside the bank."

While we spoke over the next hour or so, he threw in a few words of wisdom along with more encouragement. I sensed he was trying to help me avoid making big mistakes in the future, so I paid close attention. I didn't know yet what those mistakes would be, but I was intent on not making them if they could be avoided.

It was a bright, sunny day. Dad leaned back on the bench to spend a minute enjoying the moment. His eyes were closed when a

baseball rolled up to our bench and softly bumped into his foot. He looked toward the ball field and saw a fourteen-year-old boy standing about 250 feet away, yelling "A little help please?" With no hesitation, Dad grabbed the ball, stood up, and threw the ball over the boy's head. The boy watched the ball sail and yelled back, "Good arm!" as he ran off to fetch the ball. Dad looked down at me, flashed his sideways grin, and let go a chuckle at his own arm strength. My mouth must have been open with astonishment. Sitting there talking with him, I had started thinking of my father as someone who had just retired, rather than still being his current age. Rubbing his shoulder, he said his arm never felt better; he hadn't been able to do that in over twenty years. After he finished watching the boy catch up to the ball, Dad said to come with him. He took off at such a pace, I had to jog to keep up with him.

Our first stop was our house, to pick up my mother. She was surprised to see us in the middle of the day. "Hello you two... what are you doing here Joe? Aren't you supposed to be on a business trip?" she asked my father.

"I guess I just missed you Honey..." Dad teased, giving my mother a kiss and a little tickle on the ribs. "...The trip was cancelled, is that okay with you?" he said, gazing into her eyes with a sheepish grin on his face.

"I've seen that look before Mr. Greenfield. What are you up to?"

"Are you ready for an adventure Baby?"

Her eyes quickly took on his shine. Grabbing her purse and unplugging the iron, she said she was ready for whatever the day

would bring.

So off we went. The next stop was the old fair grounds, where they had just opened for the summer season. At first, I thought how lucky we were that the fair was open. Then, I realized my father would not have left that up to chance. We bought our tickets and enjoyed the rides and games as we had so many years ago. Just like the first time, after a few rides, most of our time was spent talking and simply enjoying each other's company.

We stayed there nearly half the day, laughing like children until our faces were sore. After we finished with the major attractions, Dad asked if we were ready for the next stop in our adventure; of course we said yes. As we neared the exit gate, we realized we still had a few unused tickets, so we gave them to a family who looked as if they weren't having much fun. When their little girl saw the tickets, she started jumping up and down in her excitement. Her parents soon caught her enthusiasm and thanked us profusely for our gift. Dad said the look on their daughter's face was thanks enough, and that was actually a gift to us. Walking through the fair's exit, I leaned over and whispered into my father's ear "compounded interest." He just smiled as he took my mother's hand.

Our next destination was a little park my mother and father used to visit when they were dating. I felt a bit odd intruding on their memory, but they seemed to take joy in explaining the memories they shared there.

My mother leaned into Dad and asked, "Do you remember how we would picnic by the big tree down by that stream?"

"Yes I do" replied my father. "And do you remember how we would make a campfire in the fire pit over by the playground Baby?"

"Yes I do." replied my mother. Then they both said in unison, "Do you remember what we would do then?" At that point they just hugged, laughing at their private memory. Yes, although uncomfortable for me again, it was nice to see them so in love and reminiscing about "the old days." Then again, with the gift of the statue in our family, it was hard to fully comprehend what were old, current or new days anymore.

Leaving the park, we headed home where my mother cooked one of her fabulous dinners. You would have thought my father was dining at a 5-star restaurant by the way he raved about her cooking. I could tell how much she appreciated the compliments by the sparkle in her eyes and the grin on her face. One thing has become very apparent to me; people react to sincere, positive encouragement. It's like adding water to the soil to help a seed grow.

After more great conversation throughout the evening, my mother left the living room to finish cleaning up the kitchen. Leaning over to me, Dad asked, "Hey son, would you mind spending the night at Jimmy's house tonight?"

I looked at him inquiringly, not understanding what he was asking. He looked a bit embarrassed and said, "Hey, don't look so surprised that I have plans to spend the evening with my bride... and if you thought the baseball throw was impressive, well..." I was embarrassed yet again, but I could appreciate how it must feel to be

back in your body when it was 20 years younger, and to be with your wife at that age too.

I picked up my jacket and walked through the kitchen, giving my mother a kiss on the cheek. "Thanks for a great dinner Mom. I told Jimmy I would come over tonight, so I'll see you tomorrow."

"Oh, okay. You sure you don't want to stay a bit longer and have some coffee?"

Dad was behind Mom and was making a shooing motion for me to leave. Embracing her in a hug, he asked, "Hey Bobby, can you give me a ride to the bank in the morning. We left my car there and I need to return an important call bright and early."

"No problem Dad. I'll swing by around seven-thirty then." I said, slowly closing the kitchen door.

As I left my parents' house, I wondered what I should do with the night. I could drive over to Jimmy's house and just go to bed, but I had a better idea. I had just spent the entire day with my father who was living one of his Banked Days. I didn't want to lose that energy, so I decided to pay Carrie a visit. By the time I arrived at her parents' house, it was getting late. When she answered the door, I just asked, "Are you ready for an adventure?"

I guess she saw the moon's reflection in my eyes. She grabbed her purse and said "Let's go."

I knew exactly where we were headed. It took almost an hour, but we were soon back at the park where I had just been with my parents. Understandably, Carrie asked, "Bobby, this is fun and all, but why are we here... late at night... in the middle of the week?"

I explained the significance of the park for my parents.
Carrie appreciates family traditions and old stories, so she indulged
me as I related my parents' history that I had learned just earlier that
day. Standing there, looking at Carrie in the moonlight, my
excitement started to build. Next to the fire pit, where I really didn't
want to know what my parents had done years before, I got down on
one knee.

"Carrie, we've known each other a long time and I can't
imagine my life without you. I can't guarantee what a life with me
will bring you, but I can guarantee I will always love you. Will you
marry me?"

Her look said it all, but to my relief, she finally did say
"Yes!" We now had our own memory of the park, built upon what
my parents had started many years ago and earlier that day.

We drove straight to tell Carrie's parents the good news.
They were very pleased, considering we had just awakened them,
but didn't seem surprised at all. I thought about swinging by my
parents' house to tell them the news, but I didn't want to interrupt
whatever they may be up to.

The next morning, I picked up Dad at seven-thirty sharp. He
was dressed and ready to go in his suit and tie. My mother stood at
the door waving goodbye. She was still in her robe, hair all amiss
and with a big grin on her face. She was embarrassed when she saw
me looking at her appearance. By seven-thirty she was usually
dressed and had breakfast cooking, and here she was still in her robe.
She dismissed me with a wave of her hand, and then waved goodbye
to her husband. As she closed the door, trying to straighten her hair,

she began singing to herself. I started to tell them the news of my engagement, but it didn't seem like the right moment.

Dad jumped into the car like a teenager who had just left the scene of his first date, and said, "Drive James." As he sat next to me, staring off into the distance, he started singing the same song as my mother.

"That's a catchy song you're singing" I said playfully.

"Yes it is. In fact, it's our new, old favorite song. We will play it at all our big moments in the years to come."

When we arrived at the bank, Dad said we had a few minutes, and suggested we go sit on the bench in the park. We settled down on the bench and he said, "Bobby, I've really enjoyed the last twenty-four hours, being with you. I've missed doing this kind of stuff together, since you got married and started a family of your own."

That came as quite a shock to me. I was still single, even though I had just become engaged to Carrie.

"By the way, you made a great choice in Carrie."

"How did you know?" I practically yelped, but then realized he had already seen this play out in the future. "So you know I asked her to marry me last night... at the park?"

"Yes, but don't hold back when you tell us tonight. While I know it now, I won't know it tonight, after I return to my future. Your announcement is one of the best memories your mother and I have, so spare no details. I wish I could live it again... I envy myself tonight... but I can tell you now... well done son... and tell Carrie not to be nervous... we are all family now. Oh, and get ready to

dance. I think our new favorite song might just be playing tonight."

I asked Dad if Carrie and I would have a son or a daughter. He just laughed and said he would keep that mystery alive for me. We spent the next hour sitting and laughing until we noticed the time. Dad said I should be getting to work and how much he had enjoyed the day. I looked over to the clock on the side of the bank and then back at my father, just as a deafening clap of thunder shook the bench. He was no longer there.

I sprinted over to the bank and caught my breath before I entered the door, I didn't want to look suspicious. Just as I opened the door, Reba was coming out to inspect the sky, which was blue and sunny. She asked where my father was, and I answered he should be along shortly. Once everything proved to be alright with the building, we went back into the bank. I didn't go to my desk. Instead, I made my way behind the tellers, past the offices, down the narrow hall, where I slowly opened the door to the small room. There was my father, sitting at the small table gathering his thoughts, enjoying his snack.

I looked at him sitting there; he looked just as I had seen him in the park. He said he was starting to remember everything, like it had been a vivid dream, with a touch of déjà vu added to the mix. I told him it was definitely real to me, and I was pretty sure Mom would say the same. I knew he couldn't know about my engagement yet, so I made sure not to mention we had just spoken about it, but I did tell him how he disappeared in the park. At first we laughed at the situation, but then we both became a bit concerned that someone may have seen him disappear. We concluded the loud thunder

probably would have distracted anyone's attention, so we chose not to worry about it.

I sat there with my father as he regained his strength. During that time, my mind drifted to the upcoming announcement of our engagement. It was interesting to hear what a monumental memory that was for my parents. I guess I had considered such an event would be more important to Carrie and me than to them. It was from that point on, that I started to look at significant events from multiple perspectives. The same occasion means different things to each person involved. For example, everyone thinks of their birthday as their special day. However, that day is just as special to their parents, but in an entirely different way. Seeing one event from multiple perspectives is similar to when branches from different trees cross. The intersecting point of the limbs is the shared moment in time. But each tree's perspective of that moment is based on the path it took to get there, and where it will go beyond that point. So tonight would be a lasting memory for Carrie and me, as well as my parents, but each of our memories would be as different as the roles we play in the event.

After Dad straightened his clothes, we went back to the lobby. The clock read approximately 2:58. Both the minute and hour hands had advanced. The day had been withdrawn.

At noon, my mother came by the bank with a picnic lunch she prepared for my father. She wanted to surprise him and say thank you for such a wonderful day, and evening yesterday. He did not feel the least bit guilty taking a long lunch with his wife, after missing the previous day with his son. Dad had learned to recognize

the importance of seizing opportunities when they presented themselves. After all, it's the accumulation of many small memories that fills each season of our lives.

As I would learn later, my father's encouragement of Mom's cooking, gave her the confidence to start a small business making and selling her jams and jellies. It started off slowly, but over the years, it became quite a lucrative business which she eventually sold for a six-figure amount. It is amazing what a little encouragement can do.

\#

An Intersecting Path:

"WWI had interrupted my years in college, but what happened after my return marked a change in my life, thanks in great part to Raymond. While he was the unofficial leader of the team, I never considered Raymond anything special for several years... but my opinion of Raymond changed on that one Saturday afternoon. Today, when I'm confronted with an important decision that could affect thousands of people, I try to remember Raymond's creativity and leadership as I formulate my solution. What he did that day, not only changed my life, but altered how the game would be played for years to come. I haven't spoken to Raymond in a long time, too long, but I consider him one of my best friends...and I know I'm not alone in my opinion."

\#

X. One for the Ages

It was early December, 1981. Thanksgiving was now behind us, and everyone was directing their focus on the upcoming Christmas season. The air was crisp, the trees bare, and you could feel an energy in the air.

Having spent the night in Belleville, I didn't arrive at the bank until mid-morning. Our bank and several in Belleville were launching a new savings campaign targeting teens. I had only been working at the bank for eighteen months, so I felt honored my father trusted me to represent our bank. We had strategy meetings all day and went out to dinner after. While the drive home wasn't that far, I thought it best to stay the night in Belleville due to the late hour and the four rum and cokes I drank during and after dinner.

I skipped breakfast so I could swing by the house for a quick change of clothes before going to the bank. While my stomach was grumbling, I finished my morning calls and was about to go out for an early lunch, when Dad and G-Pa-Frank came into my office.

"Bobby, have you caught up with your calls yet?" Dad asked.

"Yes, just finished. Oh, hi G-Pa-Frank. Hey, I'm going to grab lunch early today... had to skip breakfast... you two want to

join me? Probably just a quick burger so I can get back."

Dad replied, "Actually, I brought in some food we can share... but we want to show you something first. Got a few minutes?"

We left my office and walked towards Dad's. He entered his office and I almost ran into his back when he stopped and picked up a bag of food and water. When he turned around and asked me to follow him, I didn't realize where we were headed until we were in the back room and he motioned for me to take my lookout post. The three of us made our way to the door of the small room. When G-Pa-Frank opened the door, I saw an old man sitting at the small table, with the blanket draped over his shoulders. I hurried in and realized it was my great-grandfather, G-Pa-Raymond, asleep at the table.

My puzzled look prompted my father to recount what had happened while I was in Belleville. "Bobby, I was at work yesterday, when I heard a loud thunderclap. After I looked out the window and saw blue skies, I knew what it was. I also knew you were in Belleville, so it wasn't you. I called my father and when he answered, we knew it could only be your great-grandfather. I waited for Dad to get to the bank, and then we hurried here to confirm my theory. I didn't call you because I knew you would be back here in time."

"Dad, I can only assume he is reliving a Banked Day. Did you know he still had one to relive? Back in time for what?"

"Yes, I knew he still had a Banked Day to relive, but I had forgotten about it. All I know is it's from when he was pretty young.

Anyway, you're here now and he should be waking up in about five minutes. We will find out then."

Over the next few minutes, I told G-Pa-Frank that I always thought the missing Banked Day had belonged to him. Dad said that was his secret when I told him my theory of banked and used days, back when I was seventeen.

We sat there in silence, watching my great-grandfather until he eventually started to move. It took several minutes, but he finally opened his eyes and raised his head. He was startled to see us there, but smiled saying, "I guess I shouldn't be surprised. The thunder gave me away, didn't it?"

When I looked at the expressions on the faces in the room, I realized this was the first time the four of us had ever been in the small room together.

After my grandfather made sure his father was feeling alright, Dad said, "I thought you might be hungry. Would you like something to eat?"

"Actually, yes I am... and I suppose you're all curious about what I've just done. Would you like to join me for lunch while I tell you what happened?"

I was the first to respond, "Yes sir, I'd love to hear about it." My enthusiasm reminded me, and probably my father too, of how I had reacted to Levi's story on my sixteenth birthday. So we spread the food out on the table and got comfortable. The old man's mind was clear and his voice strong, as my great-grandfather Raymond told us his tale.

#

It all started when G-Pa-Raymond banked his second day, during his senior year of college, where he met my great-grandmother. We have always known her as Nan, but her given name was Peggy. They attended a small college, 125 miles north of O'Fallon.

Back then, Raymond was of medium height, but had thick, strong legs, equipping him perfectly to be the running back and kicker on the varsity football team. The team was called the Wildcats, and they had not won a game in their last two seasons. Raymond loved the game of football, but hated losing. He banked the Saturday when the last game of the season and of his college career would be played, because he couldn't stand to lose one more game. He used to tell me it would be well after he graduated before the team would finally win a game.

When he returned to his Banked Day, he only had a couple of hours with Peggy before he was to meet the team for pregame warm-ups. He considered skipping the game, but reluctantly went at Peggy's encouragement. All too soon, it was time to go to the stadium for the game. Peggy entered the stands dreading how the evening would likely be, after another loss. Raymond was now in the locker room listening to the same old losing game plan he had heard many times before.

It was 1920, World War I had ended almost two years before, but the country was still trying to return to normal. The Wildcat football program had been suspended during the war and this season was as forgettable as those they didn't play. Raymond only had one year left in school when he went off to fight, and now he was back to

finish his last year of college and his football career. He couldn't wait for the year to end so he could get on with his life.

Raymond was a senior and team leader in the eyes of most of his fellow players, but not to the head coach. He found himself sitting on a bench next to his old teammates, all staring at Coach Riggins. It was Coach Riggins' last season with the Wildcats, and he was anxious to get the season over with so he could retire. He thought his career was finished when the program had been suspended, but the athletic board threatened his retirement pay if he didn't coach one more year while they searched for a new coach. Raymond didn't like or respect Coach Riggins, but he was close with his running back coach, Coach Shulahan. Raymond and Coach Shulahan had often talked about ways to change up the offense to be more competitive, but Coach Riggins didn't want any change so late in his career. At any rate, this game was going to be the same as all the others, and Raymond was just going through the motions until he could spend more time with Peggy.

The Wildcats took the field with little acknowledgment from the fans, and the game started like all the rest. The Wildcats got the ball first, played three downs, and punted. The latest team to likely chalk up a win against the Wildcats was the Cowboys from St. Louis. The Cowboys took the ball and marched down the field to score a quick touchdown. The Wildcats got the ball again, tried three running plays right up the middle, and again punted. Raymond had entered the game with only 235 total yards from the previous eight games in the season. He was hoping to get fifteen more yards so he could hit the 250 mark, but it looked doubtful. The next time

the Cowboys got the ball they settled for a field goal.

This pattern repeated itself into the second quarter, and the score was quickly 24 to 0. The Cowboys were leading and had the ball on their own 35-yard line. With less than a minute to go in the first half, the Cowboys' quarterback fumbled the exchange with the center and the Wildcats recovered the ball on the 33-yard line. Because there was so little time left in the half, Coach Riggins actually called a passing play and the Wildcats were able to advance the ball to the 14-yard line. The passing game was still fairly new to football and teams usually only threw out of desperation. The Wildcats were running out of time, but the field goal squad got on the field quickly enough to successfully kick a field goal. Wildcat fans typically didn't pay attention to the game; instead they would make their after-game party plans in the stands. However, the field goal at the end of the first half actually brought a few cheers. The score was 24-3 when the Wildcats went to the locker room. At least it wouldn't be a shut-out.

While Coach Riggins gave the same old half-time pep talk, Raymond had an idea. He had been encouraged by the faint cheers from the fans and decided to do something different with the last thirty minutes of his football life. Over the coming years, Raymond became a student of the game. He spent many of his future afternoons listening to games on the radio, and later watching them on television. He had witnessed practically every major technique and strategic advancement in the game. It was going to take ingenuity and a little luck to win this game, but he now had over sixty years of football knowledge to offer.

Raymond quietly approached Coach Shulahan and said he wanted to talk with him. They snuck into a side office and Raymond closed the door.

"Coach, I know we've talked about this before, but now is the perfect time to try something new."

"Raymond, if it were up to me, you know I'd give it a try... but Coach Riggins isn't going to go for it. The old dog just isn't willing to learn any new tricks, especially with just half a game left in his coaching career."

Raymond wasn't deterred; he picked up a piece of chalk and quickly diagramed their basic running formation on the blackboard. Then he turned and said in an excited but hushed voice, "Coach, if we line up like normal, but then offset one of the backs, like this..." Raymond drew a curved line indicating how the back would take a nontraditional route, "... we could quickly toss him the ball. The defense would be caught completely off guard. He could run twenty yards, maybe more, without being touched."

Coach Shulahan stepped forward, inspecting the diagram. Raymond knew he was actually considering the play because Coach had his arms crossed and he was scratching his chin, like he always did when he was deep in thought. "Raymond, this looks pretty good... but the team hasn't practiced it. We would look foolish if we tried it for the first time during an actual game."

"Coach, if you haven't noticed, we're looking pretty foolish out there already. What do we have to lose?"

Before they could settle on what they would do, they could hear the team clearing the locker room. It was time to take the field

for the second half.

The Cowboys got the ball first and marched down the field for another field goal, making the score 27-3. Coach Riggins called the same three running plays up the middle, and it was time to punt again. While the Cowboys had their next possession, Raymond pulled his quarterback and center over for a conversation. Chris was the center, and Rick the quarterback, but Rick really preferred to catch the ball. Unfortunately for Rick, his father was an alumnus who made large donations to the college and always wanted his son to be the QB. He used his influence to force Rick into that position, causing strain in their relationship.

Raymond made sure they were away from the coaches and pulled them in close. "Rick, Chris... are you as fed-up with this crap as I am?" His teammates slowly nodded their head in agreement, just the reaction Raymond was looking for. "We have a choice here guys. We can just go through the motions, running Riggins' plays, and let this game and our season end... or we can shake things up a bit and have some fun."

This caught Rick's attention. He was receptive to anything that could change the losing formula. Plus, he really didn't care what coach or his father might think; in fact, he rather enjoyed the thought of making them mad. "Raymond, I've seen that look in your eye before, and it usually spells trouble. But this time you can count me in. What about you Chris?" Chris was a big, simple, but loveable guy. He usually went along with whatever everyone wanted to do, and with only a little protest agreed to the mutiny.

Raymond drew up a few new plays in the dirt and assured his

friends they would work. As they quietly moved back to the rest of the team, Raymond was trying to convince himself as well.

Somehow the Wildcat defense held the Cowboys, and the ball went back to the Wildcats on their own 30-yard line.

As Raymond was running out onto the field, he caught Coach Shulahan's eye and gave him a wink. Coach was nervous and tried to call Raymond over, but he pretended not to hear and took the field, huddling the team. The first play called was the standard run up the middle. Rick was under center, with Raymond behind him. Before the ball was snapped, Rick turned his head toward Raymond and nodded. Rick then left his center, going in motion to take the wide receiver position. The Cowboy's defense was confused when Chris snapped the ball directly to Raymond. He ran the ball off tackle and gained 15 yards. The defense was standing around pointing to each other wondering what had just happened. Coach Riggins had been distracted and had not seen the beginning of the play. He only saw Raymond being tackled and thought his run up the middle had finally worked.

When Raymond huddled up the team, everyone was as confused as the defense. Raymond's counterpart in the running game was Brett, who was also a senior and was excited with the off-the-wall play. "Rick, I don't know if that was planned, but it was fantastic. We should call that the 'Wildcat Formation.' Let's do it again!"

Rick looked over to Raymond and said, "Guys, listen up. We are going to play this half different than we have all year. Raymond is going to call some plays, and they are going to seem strange, but

give them a chance. Hey, if we keep doing what we've been doing, we won't win this game. We have to try something new. So what do you say... are you with us?"

The team was a bit hesitant, but excited for a change. Brett spoke up first, "Raymond, just tell us what to do and where to go, and we'll give it a try."

Raymond seized the opportunity and drew up a play in the dirt. The team asked a couple of quick questions and soon they all nodded their heads in agreement. Rick broke the huddle, calling the snap count, "Ready, hike on two."

The next play lined up the same traditional way, before Rick once again sprinted out to the wide position. On the second count, the ball was snapped to Raymond who started to run off tackle again. This time the defense was ready for him and had plugged the hole. Raymond changed directions and rolled outside; he saw Rick running down the sideline. Raymond squared his shoulders and threw the ball as far as he could. Rick was wide open and ran under the ball. He had to wait on the ball since he had outrun Raymond's arm, but he was so open he was still able to catch it. He ran into the end zone for the Wildcat's first touchdown of the game, and only the fifth of season.

It was hard to tell who was more stunned: Raymond, Rick, the Wildcat fans, the Cowboys' players, or the Wildcat coaches; but it didn't matter. The extra point made the score 27-10, and excitement was in the air. The Wildcat defense was fired up and took the field, determined to keep the Cowboys from scoring again.

When Raymond and Rick made it to the sidelines, Coaches

Shulahan and Riggins grabbed the boys for a heated discussion. The rest of the offense kept an eye on the conversation, trying to look inconspicuous while sitting on the bench. They could tell Riggins was blowing his top, his face was red and the veins in his neck and forehead were bulging. Then Coach Shulahan pointed up to the scoreboard, presumably telling Riggins that the new plays had at least produced points. That would be hard to argue. By the end of the discussion, Coach Riggins had given up. It was the last game of his career and he was ready to retire, so he conceded to let Coach Shulahan take the blame when this went wrong. The school board had wanted him to do something different with the football program; well, now they got their wish. Coach Shulahan was nervous, but he could not argue with the results he saw. He pulled the offense together and let Raymond and Rick fill them in on their assignments.

The Wildcat defense gave up a couple of first downs, but finally forced the Cowboys to punt. The third quarter was nearly half over when the Wildcats' offense took the field. This time Raymond and Brett were in the backfield as running backs. The ball was snapped directly to Raymond who ran an option play, which was still new to the game. Just before Raymond was hit, he pitched to Brett who ran for over twenty yards, thanks to a downfield block by Rick. The next play the ball was snapped directly to Rick who then threw the ball to Brett for another big gain. In just seven plays, the Wildcats scored again with Raymond gaining good yardage on each of his three runs; the score was now 27-16. The ball was snapped for the extra point try, but Raymond's kick was blocked. Even missing the kick, the Wildcat fans were going crazy in the stands.

Peggy's girlfriends were all telling her how well her boyfriend was playing. Peggy enjoyed the attention and was very happy that Raymond and the team were doing well. However, she expected the Wildcats to lose and hated to think how disappointed Raymond would be, again.

The Cowboys took the kickoff and mounted a methodical drive, mostly running the ball which consumed the majority of the time left in the third quarter. It was now first and goal for the Cowboys on the Wildcat 8-yard line. Raymond felt as if he was back in combat and he needed to motivate his troops. He asked Coach Shulahan to call a time out.

Coach called his defense to the sidelines. He also called in the offense, and when the entire team was assembled, he turned it over to Raymond to speak to the team. Looking each player in the eye, Raymond said, "Men, what we have done so far is outstanding, and no one will blame us if we lose this game. We've already exceeded everyone's expectations, except mine." Raymond looked around at his teammates. No one's head was hanging down. They were all attentive and fully focused, practically at attention. Raymond continued, "We will only, truly, live this day once, so let's do it right. Now I expect our defense to keep the Cowboys out of the end zone, and I expect our offense to drive down the field and score, and score again, until we win this game. Now what I want to know is, what does the rest of this team expect?"

There was silence among the team until Rick yelled, "I expect victory!"

Slowly, others repeated the response one by one. Raymond

saw the team's emotion rise and motioned for them to all put a hand in the center of the huddle. Raymond said, "Victory on 3: 1, 2, 3…" and the entire team roared "Victory!"

The defense took the field charged up and forced the Cowboys backwards six yards over the next three plays by stopping each run attempt in the backfield. However, the Cowboys kicked a field goal to go up 30-16.

The Cowboys kicked off and Brett was able to run it out to the Wildcats' 32-yard line before he was tackled. The Wildcats ran their option play twice, picking up a total of eighteen yards, placing the ball on the 50-yard line with just one minute to play in the third quarter. In the huddle, Raymond drew up a play in the dirt. Rick, Brett and the rest of the team looked at him like he was crazy, but they agreed to run the play. Rick took the snap from Chris and dropped back to pass it deep. Raymond threw a great block to keep the blitzing linebacker from reaching Rick. Just as Rick drew the ball back to pass it long, Brett came behind him and grabbed the ball from Rick's hand. It was the "Statue of Liberty" play," although no one would call it that for years to come. The Cowboy linemen thought Rick still had the ball and tackled him empty handed. In the meantime, Brett hid the ball on his hip until he rounded the corner and was finally tackled on the Cowboy's 20-yard line. The Cowboy coaches called a timeout to protest, but the refs ruled that it was a legal handoff. The timeout gave Raymond time to draw up a new play in the dirt and to have a quick chat with the Line Judge.

The ball was snapped to Rick who quickly threw it to Raymond, lined up as a wide receiver. However, the ball hit the

ground before it reached its mark. Raymond picked up the ball and slowly headed back toward the huddle. When the Cowboys' defense was returning to their own huddle, Raymond turned and sprinted the twenty yards to the end zone untouched. Since the Line Judge was aware of the play, he carefully watched to ensure the pass went backwards and didn't blow the whistle. The backwards pass was considered a lateral, and therefore a live ball. The Cowboys' coaches were complaining again as the scoreboard changed to 30-23, with the successful extra point kick.

While the Wildcat defense was on the field, Raymond was on the sidelines cheering for his team. Between plays, a cool breeze swept across his sweaty jersey, giving him a chill that reminded him where and when he was. Raymond stepped back from the sideline and looked around, taking it all in. His senses came alive as he cherished the game noises, the sight of his young friends' excitement, and even the pain in his legs and his bruised shoulder. He looked into the crowd and was able to find Peggy. It didn't surprise Raymond to see she was watching him instead of the game. He was the reason she was there, not the game. They exchanged smiles just as the Cowboys scored their field-goal. As the crowd cheered the Wildcat defense for limiting the damage, Raymond's focus had to return to the game. He was eager to spend time with Peggy, but that would have to wait. He strapped on his leather helmet, paying fond attention to the creaking noise it made as he buckled the chinstrap, and eagerly awaited his chance to take the field again.

The Wildcats and Cowboys exchanged scores, with the

Wildcats drawing closer as a result of their touchdown versus the Cowboys' field goal. The score was 33-30, but there were only fifty-two seconds left in the game. The Cowboys were feeling confident they would win by just fielding the Wildcats' kick off and running out the clock, since the Wildcats had no time-outs left. As Raymond was running up to kick the ball to the Cowboys, he nodded to Brett who was lined up near the sideline. Raymond squibbed the kick so it only went fifteen yards, which was recovered there by Brett before the confused Cowboys players realized what was happening.

With only forty-six seconds left and no timeouts, Raymond called two plays that were based off a combination of a crossing-pattern, the Flea-Flicker, and the Hook-and-Ladder. The Cowboys were confused but they had stopped the Wildcats on their four yard line by ridding Raymond out of bounds. As Raymond hit the turf, all the Wildcat players and coaches immediately looked up at the clock: it showed 00:00. Time had expired.

When the tackler pulled himself up off of Raymond, all the frustrations from the game got the better of him and he delivered a quick but violent kick to Raymond's ribs. The referee saw the infraction and immediately threw a flag. While time had expired on the game clock, the game could not end with a defensive penalty. The ball was moved half the distance to the goal, and placed on the two yard line for one final, untimed play. The old man in Raymond wanted to stay on the ground, but his youthful body quickly rose and he took the field holding his cracked rib.

There was little time to decide what to do. Kicking the short

field goal would tie the game. The Wildcats had not even tied a game in two seasons, but Coach Shulahan could sense this was the beginning of a change in the entire Wildcat football program, not just one game. A tie would not do this game justice. Coach motioned for the offense to stay on the field, to go for the touchdown and win the game.

Raymond saw Coach's call and said to Rick, "Look at that. I think Coach Shulahan is getting the idea now."

Rick huddled his team and they took the line. Rick took the snap and rolled right, it was the option play. He could see the Cowboys had Raymond well defended, so he faked tossing it to him and cut up toward the goal line. The Cowboys' linemen converged on Rick in a huge pile of players. The referees ran in to uncover the pile. The game was on the line. Finally, they got down to Rick and marked the ball; it was three inches short of the goal line. The Cowboys had stopped him, and won the game: 33-30.

The Cowboys players went crazy, jumping up and down while they ran to their bench. The crowd was stunned. Momentum had been all with the Wildcats. How could they have lost? The Wildcat players started to walk towards their sidelines with their heads down once again, when Raymond ran up to a dejected Rick and lifted him high in the air in a big bear hug. The team turned to hear Raymond congratulate Rick on a great game. The other players came over to Raymond and Rick, and were soon joined by the defense and coaches from the sidelines.

Raymond let the remaining Cowboy players move out of the way and then addressed his team. "Rick, Chris, Brett, defense, all of

you guys… we did something new and different today… and we were able to make a game out of it when no one gave us a chance. Sure this will go in the books as another Wildcat loss, but everyone who was here today knows it was a Wildcat Victory!" The fans soon joined the team in a goal-post destroying celebration.

Raymond took a moment to recognize the significance of the situation. In his four year football career with the Wildcats, there had never been any reason to celebrate. This could be the beginning of something new and exciting. For the first time, Raymond felt he would actually miss playing football for the Wildcats.

When the Wildcats finally got to their locker room, Coach Riggins got up to address the team one last time. Everyone waited to be scolded for not following his game plan, especially since they had lost. He cleared his throat and sternly told the team, "That was the craziest game I've ever seen. I would never have called a game like that. But it sure was fun to watch." Everyone stood there not knowing how to interpret Riggins' remark, until they saw his wink, then everyone let lose a victorious cheer. Coach Riggins continued, "My coaching career ends today, but I'm turning the Wildcat reigns over to a good man, Coach Shulahan."

All the players cheered both coaches. Coach Shulahan said he thought they may just be onto something here and couldn't wait to get to spring training for Rick's senior year. He then handed out two game balls.

"I want to give out the first game ball to the entire defense, for stopping the Cowboys in the second half." He tossed the ball to the defensive captain who shared it with his cheering teammates.

"I want to give the second game ball to a young man who showed leadership, confidence and an incredible love and knowledge of the game. This goes to Rick." He tossed the ball to Rick and the first one there to congratulate him was Raymond. Rick was sure Coach was talking about Raymond and he was about to say something to share the honor, but before he could speak, Raymond led a cheer. "Here's to Rick, Hip-Hip..." and the entire team responded with "Hooray!" The team engulfed Rick and the after-game party began.

As the players eventually went about their post-game routine, Coach Shulahan pulled Raymond to the side. He told him the real game ball should have gone to him for mixing up the plays. Coach wished he had listened to him earlier in the season, although Raymond knew a conversation then would not have made a difference. Coach hoped Raymond wasn't too disappointed, but he knew Rick's father would be so proud of Rick; he couldn't miss the opportunity to strengthen their relationship. Raymond told Coach he thought he made a good decision, as he looked over to Rick's locker and saw Rick and his father joyfully recounting the game.

After the team left the locker room, they were greeted by dozens of fans who wanted to keep the party going. The favorite after-game hang-out was the local pub. So naturally the crowd flowed through the streets the short distance to the pub. Soon the bar and every seat at every table were filled. Raymond finally found Peggy at a back table and joined her with a strong hug, lifting her up and spinning her in circles. Peggy was thrilled Raymond was in a good mood after the loss. This only made her feelings for Raymond

stronger. She could sense while the day marked the end of Raymond's football days, perhaps it was the beginning of their future. Raymond couldn't take his eyes off Peggy's smiling face. The game was fun, but seeing her again was priceless. Sitting at that table, he saw the same look in her eyes as she had at their wedding and the moment Frank was born. Knowing their future made that moment incredibly special and yet oddly familiar.

After a while, and several beers, Rick found Raymond and Peggy in a corner booth. He called several teammates over and said he had an announcement. "Coach Shulahan couldn't find Raymond after his assistant coach told him the good news, so he asked me to pass it on. Raymond ran for 108 yards in the game today!" Raymond's teammates cheered him and slapped him on the back.

Rick continued, "Hey, listen up. By running for 108, Raymond receives the 100-yard patch to go on his letter jacket." This was a big honor and everyone in the pub cheered for Raymond, teammates and fans alike. Peggy took the patch from Rick's hand and pinned it on Raymond's jacket. They shared a big kiss, to the delight of everyone in the pub.

The party continued well into the night. Eventually, Raymond took Peggy back to her dorm and said goodnight just before sunrise. Walking away from the dorm, his joy of the evening suddenly disappeared as he realized this would be the last time he would see Peggy. She had died a few minutes after Frank's birth and would be gone when he returned to the future. He desperately looked back in time to see Peggy closing the dorm's front door. He caught her eye and she gave him a coy little smile as she shut the

door. He wanted to grab Peggy and do something to change her future, but she had given birth to their son and Raymond knew she would never want to do anything to jeopardize that. So he let the door close, ending that season of his life forever.

Raymond was tired and didn't really have anywhere to go, so he returned to the stadium to relive the game, his last game. He drifted off to sleep just minutes before he returned to the future...

#

"...and that was just before I woke up here, in this room, with all of you staring at me."

Dad, G-Pa-Frank and I were sitting on the floor, looking like monkeys with our mouths open. Finally G-Pa-Frank said as he wiped his eyes, "Dad, that's the most incredible story of a Banked Day I've ever heard, and certainly better than any I have used."

Then my curiosity made me ask, "I know you just returned from living the day, but can you remember any details of what happened later? What happened to the football team the next year? Whatever happened to Rick? What made you decide to relive your day now? Honestly, I thought you were finished with our gift."

"I don't know Bobby; let me think... that's still a bit fuzzy. Well, I remember I woke up yesterday and went outside to fetch the newspaper... there was something about the feel of the cool air, or maybe some smell... I'm not sure. Anyway, that threw me back to my football playing years."

He was staring at the ground, trying hard to put the pieces of his memory back together. Slowly, he resumed telling us his thought process.

"Thinking about football made me remember the early days of dating Peggy. I suppose I just had an overwhelming need to see her again. As you all know, the last time I used a Banked Day had severe consequences. I didn't even think about my last day for all these years, but I guess the feeling I had yesterday was just too strong to ignore. So I came to the bank and quietly made my way back to the room here. Well, I was quiet, but I forgot about the thunder didn't I?"

My great-grandfather stood up to stretch his legs after the long story, and while his mind was clear and sharp, he had to steady himself against the wall. "Whoa, my legs aren't as strong as they were yesterday, even after the game. Maybe I should sit down again." After he settled in at the table again, he slowly told us of what happened later in time.

G-Pa-Raymond remembered how the Wildcats won six of their nine games the next season. Rick split his time between quarterback and wide receiver, and the option play was a staple of their game plan. Rick even played a couple of years in the fledgling National Football League, making $50 a game, which was good money back then. Then he went to law school, and after a successful career as an attorney, was elected to the state senate. Many credit his football popularity for getting elected, but all agree he was one of the best senators the state ever had.

"You know boys," G-Pa- Raymond said to all of us, "I really am proud of that silly 100-yard patch. That game was one of the best times of my life... but Frank, the time I had with your mother, as short as it was, really defined my life. I wish you could have

known her. Ah, it was sure nice to see my Peggy again."

After a while, we left the room, all four of us together there, for the first and last time. Our way down the narrow hall was slow, but soon we were standing in the back room of the bank, with the sliding wall closing behind us.

I thought G-Pa-Raymond had been caught in the closing wall when I heard him yelp, "Oh my God! Now I remember."

We all turned toward him and my father reached out to steady the old man. "G-Pa, are you alright? What's the matter?"

G-Pa-Raymond stood there for a moment and then slowly turned to my father, "Joe, can I borrow your phone book?"

Although we were all confused, Dad nodded his concurrence and we tried our best to walk calmly to his office. Once there, Dad retrieved the phone book from his bookshelf and handed it to his grandfather.

G-Pa-Raymond's hand trembled while he flipped the pages, and froze when he saw the name that had never been there before. "His name is here" his voice breaking with emotion.

G-Pa-Raymond grabbed his son's arm and with some hesitation asked, "Frank, have you heard from Claude lately?"

"Sure. That son-of-a-gun beat me at golf just last Saturday. He birdied the 18th and I shot a bogey. Some things never change."

"Well I'll be damned!" G-Pa-Raymond yelled. "It actually worked!" He pulled his son Frank up from his chair and practically danced a little jig with him. When G-Pa-Raymond saw the confusion on everyone's face, he closed the door and asked us to sit down so he could explain what happened.

"This is going to shock you all since you have lived your entire lives with your perception of history… but what happened on my Banked Day changed things. I'll tell you how history was first written, and you can remind me what changed since."

G-Pa-Raymond went on to tell us how Frank and Claude had fought over Dorothy when Frank used his Banked Day after the war, and how Claude had then joined the Marines and died in the Pacific.

Frank said he did indeed go back to that Banked Day, but he didn't go into the general store as the Greenfields had never been welcomed there. He spent the entire day with his friends.

G-Pa-Raymond asked Frank how he met his wife, hoping it was still Carolyn that he married. Frank confirmed he had indeed married Carolyn, having met her at a party Claude threw for him on his return from the war. In fact, Carolyn and Frank had a double wedding, with Claude marring Dorothy.

G-Pa-Raymond looked down and said to himself, "Claude married Dorothy eh? So they really did have something going on. Well that's fine. I'm happy for them."

My father asked G-Pa-Raymond how he had been able to change the future, from his Banked Day in college. It turned out that Raymond had written a letter which he dropped in the mail box on his way to the stadium before the game. It firmly told Dorothy's father, the town's new general store owner, that Raymond had been swindled during a recent purchase. He knew it would infuriate the proud store-keeper; that his good name should be in question. Raymond also knew he would hold a grudge, but for how long was the question. The hope was he would never let his daughter, who

was yet to be born, date a Greenfield after the insult. If it worked, there would be no fight, Claude would follow his original path in the war, and he would return home alive. It had worked.

My great-grandfather had to sit down since his legs were literally shaking. He closed his eyes and allowed himself to remember all the years that had just changed. Finally he said, "Bobby, I now remember the answer to your question... why I finally cashed in my last Banked Day." He turned to his son; took Frank's hand and looked at him with moist eyes, "Frank, Claude's death haunted you for all these years. We went for a walk the other day and you confessed to me that you couldn't sleep anymore. Nightmares of Claude's death haunted you each and every day. It broke my heart to see you that way, so I thought of this plan and decided to take the chance to change history and remove your pain. I guess we lost a good customer, but I'm so glad I was able to do this for you... and for Claude too. I love you son."

Frank replied, "Dad, based on your story, I don't doubt how horrible I must have felt. You are right, that would have driven me crazy... but I can honestly tell you that from my perception now, I never had those nightmares. I'm okay. Claude is fine. We've been best friends for years. I'll never be able to thank you enough for saving him and releasing me from my guilt. I love you too."

We stayed a bit longer in Dad's office discussing the incredible day. Finally G-Pa Raymond said he should go home and rest from all the excitement. We walked through the lobby together, where I noticed the hands on the clock had finally moved forward, reflecting the missing day had been used. Then I motioned for G-

Pa-Raymond to come over to a newspaper clipping that was framed and hung on the wall in the lobby.

"G-Pa-Raymond, I know you just relived that football game, but to us, you have always been a football hero."

"Hero? What are you talking about Bobby?"

I pointed to the clipping and watched as he read the story that had been published in the O'Fallon newspaper years ago, about what happened after that season:

> Raymond Greenfield was honored today when he was recognized by the Illinois Collegiate Football Association (ICFA) for his contribution to the game of football. "Greenfield's innovation changed the way the game has been played to this very day" said the collegiate Hall of Fame coach Robert Shulahan in a statement after the ceremony. "I was very happy when Raymond agreed to act as a consultant after he graduated. He had a full-time job, but always made time to come back and help me game-plan before each season and the championship games. We couldn't have won the National Title three years in a row without his help." Greenfield was joined by his family as he received his Medal-Of-Merit award...

G-Pa-Raymond shook his head as he read about his accomplishments, probably at the same time his memory was catching up with him. I patted him on the shoulder and offered my congratulations, "I wasn't around the first time you were honored, but I'm glad I could be here for you this time."

As he cleared his throat, he quietly said, "Thank you Bobby. That means a lot to me. I think Peggy would have gotten a kick out of this, considering how most of my college career went. Seeing her again was wonderful, but it makes me miss her more than ever."

My great-grandfather had an odd expression as he left the bank. Walking under the Christmas lights that lined our quaint downtown street, he looked as if he had just ridden the best ride at the fair and now realized it was time to leave, having spent his last ticket.

#

An Intersecting Path:

"If I'm being honest, I have to admit I'm jealous of Bobby. Bobby has great parents, a great wife, and a terrific son. Plus he owns his own business and seems to be doing well financially. We were equals growing up and going through school together. There was no reason to think we wouldn't end up in the same general position later in life. But there was a point somewhere along the way, where our paths must have taken different directions. Don't get me wrong, Bobby is still my best friend. Well, actually he is my only friend. I just wish I could have seen exactly where our paths split, because I'd much rather be where he is than where I am now. I think I had my chance and blew it, without even knowing how or when it happened."

#

XI. My First Withdrawal

Years passed, and I found another one of my father's predictions, or memories actually, had come true. Carrie and I were married and very happy, living in a small house on West 4th Street, just a few miles from my parents' home. We had been married almost fifteen years when I got bad news. My best friend since childhood, Jimmy, had died. He had been sick for the last year or so, but recently his health had declined quickly. He never married and was a bit of a loner. In my mind, he had never lived up to his potential, but he had always been a good friend to Carrie and me.

When such news comes to you, I think it is natural to wonder what more you could have done. I'm sure the nurses in the hospital would agree that my visits to Jimmy were probably just as frequent as those typically made by close family members. Still, it killed me to think of any lonely minutes Jimmy may have spent, when I was off tending to my daily routine and obligations. I couldn't go back to those regrettable moments, so I had to console myself by knowing he appreciated each and every visit I was able to give him. Each one was a gift of friendship, more valuable than anything else.

Two days before Jimmy's funeral, I had been thinking about

all the great adventures we shared. We grew up together; I had known him since elementary school. He was with me when I learned to ride a bike, when we went to our first day of school, and that day at the fair. Each summer during high school and college, we used to take a trip to the beach along the Gulf of Mexico and camp in the dunes. We called it our ACE: short for Annual Coastal Extravaganza. Still, the best times were during the perfect summer before our senior year of college.

Like electricity running through my body, it hit me. It was obvious. I would withdraw my Banked Day from the summer of 1979.

I told Carrie I needed to go off for a while to collect myself before Jimmy's funeral. Carrie, being a very understanding wife, encouraged me to take the time. I called the bank and told them the same plan. As far as anyone knew, I was going to revisit the places where Jimmy and I went camping when we were young.

Early the next morning, I packed my things for camping and headed out of town. Once I was sure I was out of sight from Carrie and our neighbors, I made my way to the bank. I parked around the corner so no one from the bank would see my car, and carefully made my way through the back door. I grabbed the blanket and pillow from the office and made my way down the narrow hall to the small room. After positioning the blanket over my shoulders and putting the pillow on the table, I was about to say the magical phrase, when I quickly stopped. I opened my bag and changed clothes from my winter clothes to cutoff jeans and a tee-shirt. My old clothes were now a little tight, but they were much more fitting

for a summer day back in 1979. Before I sat down, I double checked the table and the statue were in alignment with their marks. Then I resumed my position, closed my eyes to concentrate on the day I had banked, and recited Timmah's phrase.

#

My next memory was looking up from my bed in my parents' home. I didn't really know where I should expect to appear. I thought I would be back in the hidden room, but it seemed I had gone directly to when and where I first had the idea to bank the day. I was in my bedroom, and it was as if I had never left. I was in my pajamas so I concluded it didn't matter what I wore to withdraw a day since I ended up in the clothes of the period. I didn't know if these realizations were significant enough to be written on the wall of the small room, but they would have been good to know.

I looked at the clock; it was eight o'clock in the morning. I had to sit there and think for a while, what time did we always meet at Jimmy's house for band practice? Ah yes, ten o'clock. Since I had some time to spare, I jumped out of bed and went into the kitchen to see who was home. My mother was there, looking so young and beautiful. She made breakfast that included toast and her special jam. This was before she started to can and sell her jam at my father's encouragement. That made me smile, but it also made me realize how complex jumping through time could be. I paid her a compliment on the jam, but I stopped short of laying it on too thick. I didn't want to interfere with the encouragement my father would give her in a few years.

I was anxious to see Jimmy, but I enjoyed sitting with my

mother and catching up on old, very old, news. It was interesting to listen to the current events of our friends, knowing how the stories would unfold. I couldn't help but offer some "insights" based on my knowledge of the future. In return, my mother seemed amazed at my maturity and understanding of human nature. I wouldn't fully know until I returned to the future, but she actually told a few of her friends about my insights. And it turns out some of it actually helped them avoid negative situations in their future, or past, depending on your perspective.

For example, my mother's best friend, Ann, had just gone to the hospital for stomach discomfort, and was released without finding the real cause of her pain. In the past, she went back to the hospital two weeks later in an ambulance, where she almost died of a ruptured appendix. Ann was rushed into emergency surgery and eventually recovered from the operation, but I remembered my mother telling my father that Ann had a chronic irritation that resulted from an infection when her appendix burst. She would be on medication for years and would suffer from the side effects on a daily basis. Knowing the outcome, I asked my mother, "Mom, how's your friend Ann doing these days?"

"Well, she's feeling better today, but earlier this week, she had a bit of a stomach virus."

I knew this was how it started. The doctors did a cursory examination, and dismissed her nausea and low grade fever as a common virus. So I pried a little deeper, "Do you know if her lower abdomen was ever sore, especially on her right side?"

Mom looked at me with a puzzled expression and asked,

"Well, I'm not sure. Why?"

"Oh, it may be nothing, but we learned about common medical ailments in school last semester. It's amazing how often something serious can be misdiagnosed, which then puts patients in danger."

That got my mother's attention, "What do you mean? What could it be then?"

"Hey, I'm not a doctor, but it could be appendicitis. If it is, it's often missed because the initial symptoms resemble a stomach virus… but it can advance quickly. If the appendix ruptures, it can cause infection and can even be fatal. There's a simple blood test they can do to confirm it, but doctors don't like to spend the money on the test."

I knew that would sit on my mother's mind. Ann was her best friend and Mom wouldn't let something like this go unaddressed. The seed had now been planted. I needed to change the topic before I went overboard and raised suspicion.

There were other issues with our friends that my mother and I discussed, but I cut them short when I noticed the clock. I wanted to stay, but decided to make an excuse to leave so I could go to Jimmy's house. I asked if I could borrow the car. Mom looked at me funny and said, "Bobby, your father took it to work this morning… like he always does. Why don't you ride your bike? Did you break it again?"

I had forgotten that detail. My parents only had one car and I hadn't bought my own yet. That wonderful purchase was still a few months away. I recovered fairly well by saying, "Ha, I was just

joking. I'm really looking forward to getting my own set of wheels. I've almost saved enough, so it shouldn't be long. Hey, look at the time... I'm supposed to be at Jimmy's house early today for practice... I really should be heading out..." By then, I was up from the table and standing at the open kitchen door, "... see ya later Mom, have a great day."

Outside and almost to my bike, I felt bad about my abrupt departure, so I decided to go back and tell my mother I had enjoyed our talk. When I opened the kitchen door, I could hear my mother talking to Ann on the phone. "Ann, I know you feel better today... yes, that's great... but listen, Ann... I want you to go back to that doctor today and insist he runs a blood test to rule out appendicitis.... Yes, I'm glad you feel better, but I just have a feeling about this Ann..."

I quietly closed the door, so I wouldn't interrupt their conversation. I hoped Ann would heed my mother's advice. The next day, back in the future, I would remember she had. Ann was spared the trauma and continued discomfort of her condition, and she never knew it. I wondered how often our lives are changed simply by taking one path instead of another, without being aware we had ever even stood at the crossroads.

Back outside, I hopped on my bike to travel the mile or so to Jimmy's house. I was amazed at my strength and then realized how my father must have felt when he threw that baseball, and spent the night with my mother for that matter. When I arrived at Jimmy's house, I was earlier than normal and he was still in bed. He typically didn't wake up until minutes before band practice. I let myself into

his house and went into his room to wake him up. He looked so young, much different than recently, withering away in his hospital bed. Now he was young, healthy and not too happy I woke him up early.

"Hey man, what time is it?" Jimmy said as he rolled over in his bed to look at the clock. "Are you crazy man, it's the middle of the night." Jimmy had a way of exaggerating when his biological clock was interrupted.

"Ah, get over it Jimmy. It's almost nine o'clock. I'm only an hour early."

"So why are you here so early, what's going on today?"

"I don't know. I couldn't sleep so I thought I'd just come by and hang out before Rob gets here. Is that cool?"

As much as Jimmy didn't want to be awake, he now was. "Yea, I guess. Hey, did you see Saturday Night Live this week? I thought my aunt was going to bust a gut laughing… but I don't know man, it hasn't been the same since Belushi and Ackroyd left the show."

That's how it started. I really was back in 1979 hanging out with my best buddy. We spent the next hour just "shooting the bull" in his room, laughing and enjoying being young with no real worries. Then we heard Rob turn the corner in his car, a beat-up 1972 Ranchero Squire. It was part car and part truck, but mostly a rusty chassis on 4 wheels that squeaked with its bad front bearings when it rumbled down the road. We could hear him coming a block away, and that made us laugh. By the time Rob got to the house, we were already in the garage plugging in the guitars and setting up his

drums. Rob jumped out of the Ranchero and looked just as I remembered him. Rob was always the good looking one in the group, or at least he thought he was. He was fit and trim, and crazy enough to do just about anything. With his dry sense of humor, he was just one of those guys who was fun to be around.

Once we got going, we spent two hours practicing our best Eagles songs. Rob and Jimmy were impressed by the new chords I learned later in my life. I also suggested a slightly different drum beat to Rob that another band later used in a remake of *Hotel California*. It gave the song a different sound, which would become popular twenty years later. We sounded better than ever. I really wanted to practice the song *Boys of Summer* by Don Henley, but he wouldn't write it for another five years.

We took a break for lunch and made peanut butter and grape jelly sandwiches in Jimmy's aunt's kitchen. We washed it down with A&W Root Beer from a glass bottle. It was a simple lunch eaten off a paper plate, but it may have been the best meal of my life.

The sun was high in the sky, and the house was heating up since it didn't have air conditioning; typical in those days. We decided to go to the quarry and take a swim to cool off. I didn't have a swim suit, but my cut-off jeans would do just fine. They looked much newer than when I saw them last in the small room, and they fit better too. The day was turning out just as I remembered many days that summer. We grabbed some towels, jumped in Rob's Ranchero, and drove to the quarry with the radio playing loudly to drown out the squeaking.

By the time we arrived, there was already a crowd of kids

sunbathing and swimming. On one end of the quarry, where the water was deepest, were several ledges the kids used to jump into the water. We went straight to the lowest ledge and each took turns jumping into the emerald shaded water. As soon as we hit the water on the first jump, we felt the heat melt off our bodies. The water was deep, with the temperature dropping the deeper we went. None of us knew exactly how deep it was, because no one had ever touched the bottom.

After a few jumps, I noticed Carrie was there with some friends. I couldn't believe how young and cute she looked. Jimmy was just getting out of the water, when I walked over to him and casually said, "Hey, take a look..." pointing across the quarry to the beach area, "...Carrie's here... and isn't that Sharon with her?" I remembered Jimmy had a bit of a crush on Sharon, but he had been too shy to do anything about it.

"Whoa yea..." Jimmy whispered, "...man, she looks groovy."

"I'm going over there to talk to them. Want to come?" I said to test Jimmy's response.

"Ah, no, I'll pass. I need to work on my dives man... but tell her I said hi... and hurry back."

I expected that response, but it didn't slow me down. I couldn't wait to talk with Carrie. I wanted to jog over, but I kept my cool and casually made my way over to the girls. I walked right up to Carrie and gave her a kiss, smack on the lips, and said hello. It wasn't anything passionate, but it was definitely not a kiss you would give a friend. She was a little embarrassed at the kiss, but

didn't seem upset. In fact, she gave me a cute little smile as her glance went from my eyes down to her feet. I then remembered we hadn't kissed in public yet, well we had now. Carrie was there with a couple of girlfriends, Sharon and Kathy. I told the girls I was with Rob and Jimmy, jumping the ledges. I could tell Sharon looked interested when I mentioned Jimmy's name, so I asked if they wanted to join us. Kathy had always been a bit of a wet blanket and never really liked Rob for some reason, so she didn't want to go. No matter, Carrie and Sharon agreed and we were soon at the ledges, taking turns jumping off the lowest level. Jimmy did fairly well suppressing his nerves around Sharon, but it was still a bit awkward.

With two pretty girls jumping off the ledge, it didn't take long before three other boys came over and started flirting with them. The toughest and loudest one was Curt. Curt wasn't tall but he was stocky and liked to show off how strong he was. I knew that once Curt turned forty his metabolism would change, and his stockiness would take on a different shape, but for now he was intimidating and butting in on our fun. The girls seemed uncomfortable and suggested we go back to the beach area to relax. Realizing we were about to leave, Curt challenged us to jump off the middle ledge, just to show off. Jimmy, Rob, and I had all done that ledge before so we took Curt's challenge, even though it had been a while, especially for me. My middle-aged mind was fighting my youthful body, but together we did it. By this time, we were drawing a crowd of kids watching and egging us on to be more daring. Then someone said to jump the top ledge. The challenge hushed the crowd in an instant. It was so quiet you could hear muted

conversations all the way across the quarry. No one had ever jumped from the top ledge. It wasn't much of a ledge at all really. It was more like a big rock positioned near the top of the quarry's wall. I knew I wasn't going to take that jump, and I could see Rob wanted nothing to do with it either, which rather surprised me. Then again, Rob was adventurous not stupid. Curt and the other boys backed down as well, after making up a lame excuse that they needed to be somewhere else. That left only Jimmy. He wasn't really the type to do something like this, but he had a wild look in his eye, a kind of gleam actually. I don't know if it was something we had talked about earlier in the day, but looking back, I think I had given him encouragement, something that had been lacking in his life.

Before I knew it, Jimmy was climbing up the cliff. Carrie and Sharon were yelling at him to come down, but he just kept going. Now he was standing on the rock we called the top ledge. He looked at me, cried a crazy Tarzan yell and did the best swan dive any of us had ever seen. His body cut into the water like a knife with just a hint of a splash. We all cheered frantically, until we realized he was not rising to the surface. There were murmurs from the crowd and a girl yelled for someone to go in after him. I was just about to jump in when Jimmy broke the surface of the water like a dolphin jumping out of the sea. I swear his knees almost cleared the water. Everyone went crazy. It turns out Jimmy was the first, and likely the last person to ever touch the bottom of the deep end of the quarry; with sandy gravel in his hand to prove it. In that one moment, Jimmy had regained and surpassed the legend status we once knew from the fair. In all the commotion, I saw Curt and his

flunkies slipping into the cheering crowd, trying to go unnoticed.

We spent the next few hours sitting in the sun around the water's edge, as kids continued to come up to praise Jimmy on his dive. "Hey man, that was a cool dive off the top ledge. Did you really touch bottom? What's the bottom like?" asked a couple of high school kids.

"Yea man, it's cool... the bottom... well, it's soft but rocky... but it's cold down there... I froze my ass off." The kid's laughed, but I could tell Jimmy was a bit embarrassed he used that language in front of Sharon. She didn't seem to mind as she just kept smiling and listening to Jimmy's every word.

Then I had a great idea. "Hey guys, we should throw a party at Jimmy's house tonight... and our band could play." I knew from talking with Jimmy that his aunt would be gone that evening, so we would have the place to ourselves. Our band had only played for a few friends before, never a big party; but after such a good practice this morning, and the perfect afternoon, I felt we were ready.

Jimmy and Rob had given each other high-fives when I first mentioned the party, but frowned when I said our band would play. Jimmy was first to respond, "Ah, man, I don't know Bobby. We haven't really knocked off all the rough edges yet."

All Sharon had to do to convince Jimmy was to touch his arm and say, "Jimmy, I'd really love to see your band play. Come on, please?" After that, Rob didn't really have a choice and he begrudgingly went along with the plan.

This was going to be great. The girls helped us do some quick party planning and told everyone to be there at eight o'clock.

Jimmy, Rob, and I left the quarry to get ready for our big debut. First, we went by the grocery store and bought chips, sodas, and a few cases of beer. Hey, it was 1979. The legal drinking age was eighteen, and we had been having beer parties since high school. I was embarrassed I didn't have any money to chip in for the supplies. In my haste to change clothes back in the small room, I forgot to grab my wallet from my winter clothes. I had put some 1970 currency in my wallet, but left it behind. I would find out later from my father that anything you wanted to take back in time with you had to be held in your hand as you said Timmah's phrase. Otherwise, you only had the belongings you owned in that time, which for me wasn't much. Maybe that should go on the wall too. No matter, Rob and Jimmy covered the costs. Then we went to Jimmy's house and setup for the party; it didn't take long. We were just young boys looking for fun so we kept it pretty basic. Putting out ice chests full of beer and soda, and a couple of bowls of chips on the table was all it took. We had just enough time to setup our band equipment in the back yard, when the first guests started to arrive.

After an hour, there must have been nearly 150 kids in that backyard. Everyone was having fun, eating, drinking and enjoying the warm summer night. At one point, someone yelled, "Where's the band?" We took that as our cue to pickup our instruments on the makeshift stage. We were just about to start, when I saw Carrie and Sharon walk into the yard. They looked like music video cuties, except there would be no music videos for another three years when MTV first played: "Video Killed the Radio Star." I smiled and

waved to Carrie as she and Sharon took a prime spot in front of us. After a few tuning-up moments, Rob clicked his drumsticks, and we broke into our first Eagles song. It was a bit shaky, but we got through it.

For our next song, we decided to go for broke. We played *Hotel California*. The crowd recognized the opening riff and went crazy. Jimmy and I harmonized better than we had ever done before, and I threw in those new cords which really brought the song to life. Then when Rob kicked in the new drum beat, the crowd really went wild.

When we finished the song and the cheers died down, someone from the back of the yard yelled out, "Hey, what's your band called?" We all looked at each other, we had never considered ourselves a real band and we didn't have a name. Looking at my friends on that summer night, the perfect name came to me. I looked out at everyone standing there waiting for our reply, and announced, "We are The Boys of Summer!" Everyone cheered, including Jimmy and Rob. No one had a clue it would be the name of a huge hit in five years, and it didn't matter. It described who we were in that moment in time. We kicked into our next song and by the time we finished it, we had just created a new legend for ourselves in the small town of O'Fallon.

Carrie was looking at me like I'd never seen her do before, or after as far as I could remember, and somehow I happened to notice Sharon was looking at Jimmy the same way. That's when it really hit me, while I was back in 1979 to relive this day, everyone else was living in the normal season of their lives. They had no clue

what life had in store for them, but I did. I took a moment to scan the group of kids in the yard. It was like looking through my yearbook, but seeing it alive. I saw Brooks who would go off to college to play rugby, travel the world and then end up as a priest in Texas. I saw Doug who left O'Fallon to do commercial property appraising. I saw Gary who moved away to pursue being a chef. And there was Sam, who had moved to Houston years ago. I don't know where everyone in the yard ended up, but for now we were all together sharing an unforgettable night in the summer of 1979.

We played a few more songs to the delight of the crowd, and the party slowly ground its way to an end. As the party was thinning, I noticed a very drunk Curt approaching Jimmy. Jimmy tucked Sharon behind him, not knowing what Curt would try. In slurred speech, Curt said, "Hey Jimmy. That was a pretty cool dive back at the quarry... that took guts man... and, ah... your band rocked too." It had obviously taken Curt a more than a few beers to work up the nerve to offer his apology.

Jimmy was surprised when Curt reached out to shake his hand. Accepting the gesture, Jimmy said, "Thanks man... it's cool... glad you liked it."

Then, in a crazy sequence of events, Curt turned to leave, stumbled over a lawn chair and was promptly thrown in the back of his friend's old Dodge truck to be taken home.

Carrie and I helped clean up a bit and told Jimmy and Rob good night. Jimmy grabbed my arm and asked, "Hey Bobby, do I still need to go camping tonight? I kind of want to spend some time with Sharon man."

"No Jimmy, it's fine. I've got it covered," realizing I could cover for my missing self that night when I got home. That's the beauty of going back to the place you were supposed to be all along. I watched Jimmy leave the backyard holding hands with Sharon, happy the rest of his day would continue to go well.

I took Carrie straight home since it was getting late, and we enjoyed a good night kiss on her parents' front porch. It was strange knowing we would be married one day, while we tenderly kissed each other. I don't know about Carrie, but my youthful hormones were going wild. I couldn't do anything to jeopardize our future together, so I thanked her for coming to the party and left her porch with a big grin on my face. I went home and got comfortable in my old bed one more time. By the time my mother checked on me the next morning, I was back in the small room at the bank, back in the future.

#

After I changed my clothes, I snuck out of the bank. I needed to get home quickly. I had to prepare for Jimmy's funeral later in the day. I figured someone had to say a few words for him since he had no family and few friends. Then a wave of panic hit me. Had I used a Banked Day to make Carrie fall in love with me? That would be a violation of the same rule my father had broken that led to Cindy's death. Would my life still be the same? I recklessly drove home and ran through the doors of our house. No one was there. I called Carrie's name, but no response. I ran upstairs, through our empty bedroom into our bathroom. Carrie was there, taking a bath. I waited to see if she would welcome me or scream

that a strange man was in her bathroom. Carrie was startled by me crashing into the room, but relaxed and asked, "Bobby, are you alright? I was worrying about you."

Hearing her voice was all I needed to know that everything was fine. I collapsed at the edge of the tub and started to sob. "I'm sorry Honey... I lost track of time... it's been a rough trip."

She thought I was distraught over Jimmy's death, but I was crying thankful tears that my life was still intact. Everything was fine; the actions of the day just reinforced her love, like my father's actions at the fair had done with my mother.

I spent the next couple of hours drafting my speech and getting dressed for the funeral. Around three o'clock, Carrie and I drove to the church where Jimmy's service would be. As we approached the church I grew annoyed at the traffic. Carrie gave me a sideways glance and said I shouldn't be surprised by the crowd. Getting closer to the church, I realized everyone was trying to pull into the parking lot. When we finally parked and entered the sanctuary, my jaw almost hit the floor. Carrie noticed and elbowed me in the ribs to make me aware of my awkward appearance. Clutching my sore ribs, I looked around. There had to be over 300 people in attendance, and folks were still trying to get in. We made our way to one of the front pews where we knew we had reserved seats. After the opening hymns, the pastor said all the words typically recited at a funeral, but Pastor Charles had a real way of replacing grief with hope on these occasions.

I had been so focused on the day I had just relived, and so full of grief for the loss of my dear friend, that I had not given

myself time to remember what happened those days and years after the party. I had lived right alongside Jimmy throughout the past, but it was just now coming back to me.

Pastor Charles started talking about Jimmy as a man of honor in the community, a man with many friends and a loving family. My memories were becoming clearer while the pastor continued. Then Pastor Charles asked if Jimmy's wife Sharon would like to say a few words. I felt another jab in my ribs when I did a double-take to see Sharon sitting in the front pew. Carrie asked me what was wrong, but I was too stunned to reply.

Sitting next to Sharon was Pastor Charles' wife, Belinda. In small towns, the pastor's wife traditionally plays a huge role in the life of the church. In this case, Belinda's compassion allowed her to be a great source of strength to grieving families. As my memory of the past was catching up with me, I recalled how Belinda had spent many days with Jimmy and Sharon at the hospital. She and Sharon had formed a true friendship, which made me wonder what other bonds had been formed, or maybe broken, since I used my Banked Day.

Belinda leaned over to Sharon and gave her a warm hug of encouragement. Sharon rose and walked up to the pulpit. She was much older, but still had the same beautiful face, although the shine in her eyes was clouded by tears. She spoke of her love for Jimmy and all the wonderful years they had together. She introduced their five children who were seated in the front row. After Sharon was finished, others were invited to come forward to say a few words about Jimmy. When I stood, I was joined by dozens of others there

to show their respects to my best friend.

To my surprise, the first person to speak after Sharon was Curt. Curt and Jimmy had become great friends, and after college had gone into business together. I recalled how I had helped them secure their first small business loan. Curt looked good. He was trim and in shape, which was much different than the way he looked when I last saw him in future-time. Curt was choked up as he spoke about his close friend and vowed to be there for Sharon and the children.

It took thirty minutes before it was my turn to speak. I threw away my notes, they didn't pertain anymore. "Jimmy was my best friend. I'm guessing many of you here might say the same thing about him, and that makes me happy." I felt myself choking up, I needed to break the tension, "I don't know about all of you, but the day Jimmy jumped off the top ledge at the quarry seems like yesterday..." that brought a smile to many in the church, "...and for those of you who were there that day, I know you remember his Tarzan yell when he took off from that ledge..." now, a slight chuckle rose from the crowd. "...and if you were at the party that night, you remember our singing wasn't much better." Everyone then let loose with a good belly laugh.

The joke didn't deserve the level of response it received, but everyone needed a bit of comic relief. I could even see a smile on Sharon's face, and Jimmy's children laughed out-loud at the story they had heard many times about their father.

I closed my remarks with genuine thanks to God that he had brought Jimmy into my life; I was a richer man for knowing him.

Walking down from the pulpit, I noticed faces that I had not seen since the party in the backyard. Brooks, Doug, Sam and Gary were all there, along with many others I had not expected. I didn't have time to recall if their futures had been changed by the events of that summer day, but I was glad they were all there. I was grateful that Jimmy's life had been filled with so many friends. It eased my guilt of not always being at the hospital for him. I now knew when I wasn't there, he had other friends and family to comfort and be with him.

As we walked down the steps in front of the church, I was reminded by the cold air that it was indeed winter; much different than the weather I had recently enjoyed. I hadn't noticed them in the church, but my parents and G-Pa-Frank were waiting for us outside. We had just joined them when Rob approached Carrie and me and said in an excited voice, "Bobby, good job on the pulpit... I mean, that's not easy to do... but I got to tell you... I had a dream last night about Jimmy's dive at the quarry... and the party after... it was so real... I thought I was really there... I mean... my hands were actually sore this morning, like I'd been playing my drums."

Others around us stopped and said they too had the same dream, just last night. That's why they reacted as they did when I mentioned it from the pulpit. Carrie smiled at me and nodded her head in agreement. Dad and G-Pa-Frank stood there smiling in silence, suspecting what had happened. We all shared something in that moment, just as we did all those years ago. In some dimension, I knew Jimmy was there too.

The next day when I returned to work, I checked the old

clock. The hour hand was now on the 13th mark. It was sad to see the tangible evidence that one of my three priceless days was over, but the positive impact from the ripple effect made it worthwhile.

XII.   Another Generation Coming of Age

Looking back over the years, Carrie and I fulfilled the other part of my father's prophecy. In 1982, our son Kyle was born. He was the sun that lit our world. Carrie had a difficult pregnancy, and we almost lost Kyle when Carrie was twenty weeks into the term, forcing her to go on bed-rest for the remainder of the pregnancy. During that time, I was reminded of the tragic outcome when Nan gave birth to G-Pa-Frank, so I was relieved when Kyle was born healthy and Carrie was fine; that's all that mattered.

We were like most young parents, trying to do the best we could at work and home, while trying to carve out time to spend with our family. With our hectic schedules, we found ourselves in a routine where we did our evening chores, politely asked about each other's day, and spent a couple of hours with Kyle. Then, we would put him to bed and sit in front of the TV to relax until our bed time. The days were long and full of work, and even the fun things were becoming chores to us. Taking Kyle to the park was included in our list of things we "had to do." It became just a task, fit between other tasks, filling the day.

For example, on Kyle's third birthday, we had a meltdown

just because we had this perspective. We planned a small birthday party at our house for Kyle and eight of his friends. Carrie was in charge of preparing the house, and I was to pick up the cake from the bakery and buy the decorations. Instead of including Kyle in my activities and making it a fun day, I tried to run my errands alone. That left Carrie with a three year old as she tried to prepare the house. Meanwhile, I was dealing with a ballerina cake instead of a Batman cake, and having to drive all the way to Belleville to get the right decorations. By the time we finally had everything ready at the last minute, none of us were in the mood for his party. We were ready for the day to end before the first guest had even arrived. That day was a lost opportunity. We let our "chores" ruin what could have been a favorite memory of Kyle's childhood.

Looking back on those days, I wish we had realized what the fun events were versus real chores, and that we had used them as rewards for ourselves. Life can be hard and we need rewards, and they don't have to be big or expensive. The best rewards cost nothing except the effort to recognize and accept them as such.

After several years of our routine, I woke up to the idea that while this might seem rather mundane to me now, a day like this could be wonderful to relive later in my life. So I made my excuses to be gone for a day, and I banked a "normal" day in this season of our lives. The clock now read two fifty-nine, or was it three fifty-nine? It was hard to tell since the hour hand was on the 13th mark.

#

More years passed, and Kyle grew to be a fine young man. His daily life wasn't really very different from what mine had been,

or my father's for that matter. Life in O'Fallon didn't change much from one generation to the next. However, I think the biggest difference for Kyle was he had the benefit of certain insights from G-Pa-Frank, Dad and me. Before he was sixteen years old, we were very subtle with our advice and leading questions. We tried to be careful and not confuse the boy with the complex nature of time, but we were laying a foundation.

Finally when Kyle turned sixteen, G-Pa-Frank, Dad and I took him to the bank to tell him the secrets of the statue. I had this day planned for quite a while. I wondered how Kyle would remember this day versus how I had when I was sixteen. This time was a bit different in that Kyle was being escorted by his father and two G-Pas. We had already discussed who would take the lead in explaining certain parts of the story, so we wouldn't step on each other's toes. We were all very excited as we entered the bank with Kyle.

Just as Dad and I had done when I was sixteen, we passed through the lobby saying hello to the tellers. We went to the back offices, and then to the remote section of the bank that led to the hidden hallway. This time I was asking the birthday boy to keep a lookout. It was like looking in a mirror when Kyle turned around to see the wall pulled back, exposing the hidden hallway. When we were at the seemingly dead-end of the hallway, Kyle was amazed when I inserted the key into the hidden keyhole and slowly opened the door to the small room.

"Dad, what the hell is this?" Kyle blurted out when the door opened. I guess that is one difference between our generations. I

never would have cursed in front of my father, but I let it go as I knew he was too excited to pay attention to details like manners. Then I was pleasantly surprised when Kyle caught his mistake and rephrased his comment, "I mean what the heck is this place?"

"Kyle, this is a special place very few people know about. It's in this small room, that you will have the opportunity to change lives. Not just your life, but others as well. That carries much responsibility, but your G-Pas and I are here to help you along the way."

We asked Kyle to take a seat at the table and we started to recount the same story Dad told me all those years ago. G-Pa-Frank got comfortable on the floor, and Dad started off telling Kyle about Levi joining the Confederate Army and his time in the prison camp. Hearing Dad's voice and seeing Kyle at the table hanging on every word, gave me the mirror imagery again. At the point in the story where Levi spent time with Timmah, we switched speakers in our tag-team approach. I wanted to explain this section because it included details from my own experience. Kyle was the first Greenfield to be told Levi's story with the added details learned from the trip to Hamburg. It had been years since Dad and I returned from our trip and told my G-Pas, so it was fun to recount it all again to someone new. As we would find out, from this point forward, Kyle would bring new and thought provoking insights about the trip and to our gift in general.

Kyle was filled with the same questions I had at his age, and my father before me. I walked him through the list of Rules, which seemed to satisfy most of his initial curiosity. Then Dad addressed

how the old clock kept tally of days banked and used. Out of nowhere, Kyle fired off a stream of questions that had both Dad and I scratching our heads about how to respond. His questions were comprehensive to everything he had heard. Each included detailed sub-questions that then rolled in to the next topic. We knew the answers to most of his questions, but we didn't know the best way to explain it to Kyle that wouldn't be confusing. Finally Dad said, "Kyle, I have to give it to you. You have more questions than either I or your Dad did when we first heard about all this. That only goes to show how smart you are. I tell you what; give us a little time to talk about how best to approach your questions. I promise we will make sure each and every one is answered, the best we can… but I will tell you this, I don't claim to know everything about this power… not yet anyway."

I agreed this was a good point to bring our initial introduction of our gift to an end. We were all tired so I said, "Kyle, I think we should stop now and let you digest all of this for a while. Today is Wednesday. Let's plan on the four of us getting together again this weekend, and we will start sorting through all your questions." We agreed to that plan, so we locked up the room, stored away the key, and walked down the hall. Just as we arrived at the secret sliding wall, Dad stopped me and looked through a peep-hole in the wall to make sure no one was on the other side.

"Dad, what the hell?" I yelled. I had never known about the peep-hole.

"What, didn't I ever show you this?" replied my father. He smiled at G-Pa-Frank as he shrugged his shoulders. "And watch

your language young man." Then my father grinned and we all laughed at my temporary slip in manners. I guess Kyle's and my generations aren't that different after all.

#

Over the next couple of years, Kyle, G-Pa-Frank, Dad and I would take many walks to discuss the power of the statue and the many what-if questions Kyle came up with. We shared how we had used our days so far, gave examples of both good and bad, and reinforced the importance of following the rules of the statue. It didn't take Kyle long before he knew enough to raise some questions we had never considered.

It was a few months before Kyle's seventeenth birthday when he started bringing up some very creative questions. Three of us were on a walk this time, and when we were well away from our house, Kyle asked, "G-Pa-Joe, I understand that we can't bank a day sooner than one year since the last day we banked, but the three of us could each bank a day in the same year, right?"

Dad looked at me and said, "I think so, although I'm not sure that has ever been tried."

Kyle continued, "Well, assuming we could, do you suppose more than one of us could bank the same day?"

I jumped in at that point, "I don't know for sure Kyle, but I doubt it. I can't imagine one of us could engage the statue while another of us already has it in use."

Then Kyle continued with the line of questioning, "Okay, that probably wouldn't work, but how about this? You told me we can take things back to a Banked Day if we hold it in our hands.

Does that only apply to objects?"

"What do you mean?" Dad asked.

"Well, what if I banked a day, and then when I go back to relive it, I took one of you with me by holding your hand?"

Dad and I looked at each other and shook our heads. Dad was first to respond, "Kyle, that's a new one alright. Well, my first reaction is it would be very risky."

Before Dad could continue, Kyle jumped in with his litany of follow-up questions, "I know it's risky. First, you just don't know if a living creature can be 'carried' along with you. Second, even if that worked, would it count as one of the other person's days? What if they didn't have any remaining days to use? Would it just leave them in the room, or would the violation of the number of days cause the person holding the statue to give up one of his days? I don't know."

I looked over at my father; he was slowly exhaling as he shook his head in confusion. I suggested, "I think I would try it with a mouse first, to see if you could 'carry' another living creature with you... and what happens to it if you are not holding it at the exact time you return to the future. I wonder if you weren't holding it, would the mouse stay in the past. I'm not sure how you could answer your other questions without the help of a family member... it all sounds pretty risky to me."

"Speaking of getting stuck in the past..." Kyle continued without hesitation. "...what if someone in our family dies in the past, while living a Banked Day? I would have to assume they are dead in all time dimensions, past and future... what happens to the clock?"

"To the clock?" Dad blurted out. "A person dies in the past and you are wondering about the clock?"

"Yea... well... I mean... dead is dead... sorry, that's just life... but one of the Rules says all days are forfeited upon death. So would the clock register the day as a completed Banked Day, with both hands moving forward? Or, would the day just disappear and only the minute hand would move up to say there wasn't a pending Banked Day anymore... and the hour hand would simply stay where it was?"

With a nervous giggle that really meant this question made me uneasy, I said, "Bobby, that is one what-if I hope we never see get answered."

We continued to talk about all the possible ramifications on this scenario for the remainder of that walk, without reaching any conclusion, but it was definitely a good exercise in what-if scenarios. My father told me later that he hadn't heard creative scenarios like that since our fishing trip with all the G-Pas.

#

It was just a few weeks later, on another walk with my father and me, when Kyle came up with this one.

"Dad, I have a question for you."

My father and I looked at each other; we knew where this was going.

"Okay son, let me have it." I responded, holding my breath.

"Well, let's say I learned something about one of you two... and it was something I couldn't really bring to you in that moment in time, for whatever reason... but I realized that if I went back to a day

I had already banked, I could tell you about it then, and you may be more receptive. I don't have a good scenario why that would be the case, but just go with me on this. Okay... so while I'm back in time on my Banked Day, you realize that you could fix something that was going to turn out bad... but you had to relive one of your Banked Days, right then and there. Would it work if you tried to cash in a Banked Day... while I was doing the same... even though technically we were doing it years apart?"

"Wow, that one made my head spin." replied my father.

I jumped in, "Well Kyle, let's say it's me you went back to see. If I thought reliving a Banked Day would help, I would probably wait until the next day to do it. That way we could spend the day together, and I could simply avoid the situation."

"Okay, that sounds right, but it didn't answer if it is possible. So how about this... what if the situation was different? This time it wasn't that you had to relive a Banked Day while I was doing the same. This time you had to bank that particular day... the same day that I went back to... could you do that? It's not like we were at the same point in time, when we both tried to bank the same day... but the statue is in the middle of a 'banking event,' so I don't know."

Dad then asked Kyle, "If I'm following all this correctly, you went back in time to tell your father something that he needed to fix that day. So, why would he need to bank that day? Couldn't he just do what he needed to do in his real-time? You could tell him all the future information he needed to equip him to make the change." Dad looked proud that he managed to keep up with Kyle.

I thought Dad had stumped Kyle, until he said, "Well, that

could be the case, but the information I would have would be from my experiences. It could be that the action Dad would need to take is dependent on something only he would know in the future. Or here's another possibility. Maybe I went back to my Banked Day and something bad happened while I was there that I didn't expect. Since I can't bank a day twice, because I would violate the 1-year-wait rule, I could ask my father to bank that day and he could fix the thing that went wrong."

I just had to laugh at that point, saying, "Kyle, I give up. You're too good at these what-if's. How about you Dad, give up?"

I looked over at my father who had stopped dead in his tracks. He pulled me aside and whispered, "Bobby, my father could have done that when Cindy died. Oh my God, we could have saved her."

I told Kyle to give us a moment, while I pulled Dad over to a large tree for privacy. My heart was racing and my mind spinning. Although I was also shaken, I tried to say something to calm down my father. "Dad, now hold on a minute. Don't blame yourself. You and your father were in shock. There is no way you could expect yourself to come up with that solution under the stress. You know Kyle has an out-of-the box way of thinking. We could try for a year and never come up with that."

"But Bobby, we could have saved her. I don't know if I can live with the guilt, now on top of my shame."

"Dad, stop it now. Even if that would have worked, we don't know what else may have gone wrong. You may have just compounded the problem."

"Bobby, your grandfather and I never spoke about that day. I know we both felt incredible guilt, but there was nothing we could do, other than punish ourselves in silence. I can't tell you the number of endless hours I've spent going over those events, looking for a way to make it all go away... and in an instant... Kyle came up with the answer. I'm so stupid. Promise me son, don't tell Kyle about my stupidity, not while I'm alive anyway. I couldn't stand him thinking his grandfather, and great-grandfather, were so simple... and never tell G-Pa-Frank, it would kill him."

After a moment, Dad seemed to compose himself, but I could tell he was just compartmentalizing all this for now. He would deal with this for a long time, maybe the rest of his life. "Dad, I won't tell G-Pa... and you know you have me to talk to about this, when you are ready." As it would turn out, we never would bring it up again.

We both stood there for a while in silence, deep in our own thoughts. Eventually, Dad wiped his cheek dry and straightened his back, saying, "It's alright son, you're right. It's not realistic to think we could have thought of Kyle's theory. That boy just thinks in ways we barely understand, much less can come up with ourselves. He is bound to add several rules on the wall during his life. You should be proud of him. Now, let's go get the boy and head home."

We rejoined Kyle who took a look at his grandfather and asked, "Are you alright G-Pa-Joe? Was it something I said?"

"Oh, I'm fine. I just had to tell your father something about work before I forgot." Looking over to me, Dad said, "I think his generation has an advantage over us. They deal in imaginary worlds

on the internet and aren't confined by our reality. Sometimes I don't think I can add much to these conversations, but I'll keep trying. Anyway, I'm ready for some of that apple cobbler your mother was baking. Let's go home and grab a slice."

Kyle took the lead on the way home as Dad and I became lost in thought. Another walk concluded as many did. Two of us with headaches and Kyle with an extra skip in his step. It seemed as if he was always one step ahead of us should-be experts.

#

Kyle went off to college to study business and landed his first job at the 1st Bank of O'Fallon. No big surprise there I suppose. Carrie and I were so proud of Kyle. As he learned the banking business, I told Kyle how my father had used a Banked Day to come back and encourage me. I told him all about that Banked Day and also shared the same business advice my father had given me. I wasn't sure if I had successfully avoided the pitfalls Dad was trying to protect me from, but I hoped sharing it with Kyle might also help him one day. Lessons learned in one generation often apply just as well to the next.

Kyle gained a real sense of integrity, which I'm very proud of. I could see it in his professional life, but more importantly, it was interwoven in his basic fabric. This was evidenced one day when we were together at a gas station. A young lady in her late teens came bursting into the store. There was no one else there, but still she jumped in front of us at the counter. She told the cashier she wanted eight dollars of gas on pump two, and then she quickly left the store to pump her gas. As the cashier was ringing up her sale,

Kyle said, "Excuse me sir, here's an extra dollar to give her nine dollars of gas."

The cashier was surprised, but took the dollar and finished the transaction. Kyle continued, "I want to see if she will stop at eight dollars."

"You like to shake things up, don't you son?" the cashier said with a smile at the little game.

"Yea, but then I don't get out much." They both laughed as the girl started pumping the gas. Watching Kyle, I could sense a change in his demeanor. This was more than just a game. I was puzzled by where he was going with this.

Looking at the pump register behind the counter, the cashier counted down her progress, "She's at seven... almost to eight... now... she's over eight... there... she finished at nine dollars... she had to, the pump automatically turned off."

We all looked out the window as the girl hung up the pump nozzle, then quickly got in her car and sped away.

I expected Kyle to make a joke, but instead he disappointedly said, "I was really hoping she would stop at eight, or at least come in when she realized she had gone over. It takes years to earn your integrity, but it's amazing how cheaply people will sell it. In her case, it only took one dollar." Both the cashier and I nodded our heads in silent agreement, as I stared at Kyle. Sometimes I wonder what goes on in his head; his brain just isn't wired like mine.

Kyle's experiment in human nature was well worth one dollar. I heard later from the cashier that he repeated the story to his coworkers, who used it as an example to their children. It made me

proud to know my son was conscious of his integrity, and was diligent not to lose it at any price.

XIII. Change is in the Air

While Nan died giving birth to my G-Pa-Frank, her husband Raymond lived into his 90's. In 1990, he passed-away just a few years before Jimmy. Their deaths marked the beginning of a difficult season in my life. Looking back on those times, I think I became slightly depressed with the realization that no matter how many times we bounce back and forth, time ultimately plods relentlessly forward. We are all predestined to the same end game: death. For some of us, death comes well before our bodies quit.

After Raymond had relived his last Banked Day to save his son a lifetime of guilt, he lost much of his zeal for living. He told me toward the end of his life, he had now seen and done it all. I took that to mean he didn't have much left to look forward to. When someone gets to that point, days, weeks, and months turn a shade of grey; colors just disappear.

But I'm happy to say G-Pa-Raymond's long and eventful life did provide him and his family with many colorful memories. I admire how he willingly served as a pioneer in the early days of our family's use of the gift. He helped lay the foundation for how we continue to use Banked Days, always with responsibility and a focus

on integrity. Still, I do wish his last years could have been more rewarding; he just seemed to fade away.

#

In the fall of 2005, we added another generation to the Greenfield bloodline. Kyle was now the proud father of Kristine Greenfield, my lovely granddaughter Kristy. I finally knew what everyone was talking about, I was a G-Pa and it was fantastic. Seeing that little girl instantly freed me of the depression I had carried since Jimmy and Raymond's deaths. I was now focusing on life again, and everyone's future seemed bright and colorful. It was interesting for Carrie and me to watch Kyle grow as a father. We tried to offer advice on the logistics of parenthood, without becoming the overbearing grandparents. Many times it was difficult to bite my tongue, but I knew certain lessons had to be learned the hard way, especially during the terrible-twos.

Kyle was devoted to his wife and daughter, but maybe more so to his career. As Kristy grew from a toddler to a preteen, Carrie and I would often attend her special events, with only her mother there with us. Kyle would be off with a client or in Belleville on business. I tried to explain to him that these days only came around once, and he should take advantage of them while he could. He never disagreed, and always said he would make it a priority, but the pattern continued. Kyle was slowly being left out of family events and I was filling the void. I have to confess, I really didn't mind. It allowed me to develop a wonderful bond with Kristy, but looking back, it was at Kyle's expense.

#

In the spring of 2007, my G-Pa-Frank died. While his passing was sad, the atmosphere at his funeral was one of remembrance and celebration, where Raymond's had been more remorseful. Having avoided his burden of guilt over Claude, Frank had lived a full life, with no regrets. I can honestly say he was my favorite G-Pa. His wisdom, combined with his playful nature, created the perfect blend in his personality. He and my grandmother Carolyn spent their golden years with Claude, Dorothy, and their families. They were inseparable, enjoying each other's company as if they were on a lifetime of Banked Days. In a way, I found Frank's death inspiring, as I did his life.

#

I saw my parents enjoy their golden years together. They went on a cruise to the Bahamas, which they could afford due to the success Mother had with her jam and jelly business. Well, at least that's what Dad told her. He confided in me that he made a ton of money in the stock market. It seems when he supposedly went to the bank on our day at the fair, he had actually gone to purchase stock in a young company called IBM. The stock's value had risen quite a bit from 1967 to 1992. Dad had taken almost all the money they had at the time and converted it to currency from the 1960's. The big wad of cash we saw at the fair was what remained after his stock purchase. He decided to leave the stock alone for twenty-five years, letting it mature into a small fortune.

Dad was clever with his finances. He made sure all required taxes were paid, but otherwise, he tried to keep his wealth quiet and not raise any flags in our community. Sure, he spent some money,

but never on frivolous purchases. Over the years, my parents remodeled different parts of their house: updating the kitchen and bathrooms, adding a study, and extensive landscaping to include a pond behind the house. Mom always enjoyed a good home improvement project, as long as she didn't have to pick up the hammer. She was a good project manager and kept the subcontractors hopping. Dad also made sure they took at least one big trip a year. He said life is too short to wait to go somewhere, someday. Mom never pried into where the finances came from, although I could tell it made her a bit uneasy. Dad was good at deflecting her concerns, refocusing her on the planning of the trip or the home improvement.

Change wasn't limited to the size of our family or Dad's bank account. My father became an activist. Dad kept an eye on worldly events, but he put his focus on charity at the local level. He had always been an active member of our church and the Chamber of Commerce, but in recent years he also became a member of the School Board and was on a special commission established by the mayor to oversee local charities.

Dad often spent his own money to help those in the community who were in financial need. He called it his Helping Hand Community Outreach, and incorporated it in the mayor's special commission. Everyone, besides the mayor, thought he had secured federal grants to fund these efforts, and that was fine with him. He never wanted recognition; he only wanted to help where he could.

#

Years ago, before G-Pa-Frank died, I can remember Dad often telling me that people who genuinely want to make a change, often bite off more than they can chew. They set their sights too high and end up not hitting the target at all. That often creates frustration and results with them just quitting. A better choice is to start smaller, where you are more likely to have success. He would say we should put our attention on what we can influence, focus on helping individuals, and let it grow naturally to helping groups. The same mistake happens when we build a long range plan, before we have taken our first step. Those plans are fraught with failure because they are not based on real-life experiences, learned from starting small.

More than once, I would argue with my father that we need to set our goals high, so even if we did miss them, we still achieved measurable success. His reply to me was our ambitions should be set high, but we should establish achievable goals and manageable plans to get there.

We continued this discussion on several of our walks. I was content for this to be one area we just agreed to disagree, but Dad was passionate he had the winning formula and wouldn't let it drop. On one cloudy Saturday morning, Dad tried a new approach to get through my thick skull.

"Bobby, if you had only one Banked Day left to use, and your intention was to use it to help others, would you spend it with family and friends or with a large group of people you don't know?"

Taking some offense at the question, I asked, "Well Dad, are you asking me if I would be so selfish that I would use the day on

my personal life versus spending it to help those I don't really know. Is that what you meant?"

"No, I don't want to make this a big moral issue... like if the good of the many is more important than the good of a few. I just want to know, where do you think you could be most effective?"

I realized I had over-reacted to his question. So with a smile I said, "That's easy. I would spend the day with family and friends."

"Why?"

"I would have a greater influence on those I already know than with strangers. So if I only have one day to help them, I have to rely on the relationships I've already established to gain their trust."

"Exactly Bobby... you very succinctly made part of my point. Now, let's say you had one Banked Day left, and you wanted to use it to help a close friend somehow. Would you come back to tell him about something that will happen in his near future, or something that won't happen for a long time?"

After thinking a moment I replied, "I think it would be most effective if he could see the results quickly, while our discussion was still fresh in his mind. Otherwise, he would likely forget about it, or let other priorities stand in the way."

"Perfect, you make a good straight man Bobby," Dad said with a chuckle. "So you just told me we should focus our attention on people we have existing relationships with, and we should have a sense of urgency so we can achieve quick wins. That sums up my overall philosophy on how we can make positive change in the world. When everyone does their small part, it adds up to something huge. We can't fix the world's problems by ourselves, but if we all

focus on solving one specific problem at a time, in our own little part of the world, it is amazing how fast things can get done. The scale of the change will become larger if the solution really has merit."

Logically, I understood Dad's philosophy, but I still resisted accepting it completely. It seemed too simple to have the world-wide change effect I was looking for.

A few weeks later, I arrived at Dad's house all set to take another walk. This time G-Pa-Frank was going to join us. He hadn't joined us in a while due to his age. As we left the house, Dad pointed to his car and said, "Bobby, climb in. We want to change things up a bit today."

I looked at him and then to G-Pa-Frank, who was just nodding his head and smiling. We drove in silence along I-64 and took the exit to the east side of St. Louis. That part of town is known for crime, drugs, and poverty. We pulled up to an old, run-down looking warehouse; with several cars parked in front and a truck backed up to a loading dock on the side of the building. My father turned off the engine. Both he and G-Pa-Frank swiveled in their seats to face me in the back seat.

G-Pa-Frank took a breath and told me why we were here. "Bobby, your father told me about how you two have been discussing the best way to make changes in this world. So I asked if I could share something with you. When I was about your age, I wanted to go to Africa to help the starving children there. We had studied their situation in school and it really left an impression on me. When I told my father about my idea, he brought me here."

"What is this place G-Pa-Frank?"

"This is a food bank Bobby. It's been around since before the Great Depression. My father, your G-Pa-Raymond, used to donate his time here whenever he could. When he brought me here, we spent the whole day helping organize the donations and taking food to the elderly in the community... and that's what we are going to do today."

I was a bit confused by what exactly we would achieve, until we made our first food delivery, to Mr. Gordon. He was well into his eighties, lived alone, and used a walker to get around. While his body was slowly failing him, his mind and spirit were sharp. We visited with him for almost an hour, which was just as important to him as the food we brought. Before we left his house, Mr. Gordon asked us to drop in on Mrs. Williams. Her hip was bothering her and she hadn't been able to leave her house to pick up groceries for a few days. We spent the rest of the afternoon making deliveries and visiting Mrs. Williams and other elderly people; as well as unwed mothers and seemingly normal families who were just down on their luck.

When we returned to Dad's car for our ride home, Dad turned to me and asked what I had learned that day. My answer came quickly as I knew this was where we were headed all day. "Well, after meeting the people in the food bank, and seeing how one afternoon of our time really did touch so many people, I understand what your father told you G-Pa-Frank, and what you have been trying to tell me Dad. We don't need to go half-way around the world to help people. They are right here, desperately waiting for us to do whatever we can. Today transformed your

philosophy into reality for me. After seeing those faces and the impact we made to these people, I can see how the food shelter has become part of the community… and that has helped make this community a place where everyone looks after each other… and the ripple effect goes on from there. This wasn't the type of bank I thought we would talk about today, but I can see where the two fit together. We've been talking about how to use Banked Days to help others, but today I discovered how we can do that every day."

Dad and G-Pa-Frank didn't say a word. As if orchestrated, they both smiled and turned in their seats for the drive home.

That day is very special to me as it was the last outing I shared with G-Pa-Frank before his death. In his honor, Dad and I have often returned to the Food Bank in East St. Louis, and as Kyle grew older we included him as the next Greenfield generation to help there.

Dad was smart enough to bring in our family's history, along with scenarios of using Timmah's gift, to convey his simple yet insightful philosophy of change to his stubborn son. Perhaps this philosophy is our greatest gift, helping us and many people in the O'Fallon area who have never even heard of Timmah.

XIV. Perspective Is Everything

The years continued to pass, with seasons coming and going on their normal schedule. Then in 2017, a significant event happened in my life; it was time to cash in the day I had banked when Kyle was small. I made my excuses to be gone for a day, and went to the small room at the end of the narrow hall. I made sure I had proper currency in hand and set up my pillow and blanket as Dad had shown me long ago. I closed my eyes and uttered those magical words.

#

When I opened my eyes, it was 1986 and I was back in our small house on West 4th Street. I walked in the front door; four year old Kyle ran up to me with his arms wide open and pure joy on his face to see me. I snatched him up and spun around in circles. His arms were tight around my neck and it felt as if he had just melted into me. The feeling was incredible. I can still feel him like that today, vivid in my muscle memory. Carrie came around the corner of the living room and looked at me as if I were crazy. I walked over and gave her a big kiss and a pat on the rump, at which she giggled like a school girl. We spent the evening playing. We played

"let's make dinner." We played "let's take a bath." We played games until it was time for Kyle's bedtime and then we played "story time." Nothing was a chore, only fun, and so rewarding. It was difficult to turn off the light to Kyle's room but he was already asleep, and now it was time for his parents to play.

In the middle of the night, while Carrie was asleep, I left our home and drove to my parents' house. I knocked on the door and Dad answered. To see him again almost made my knees buckle. I asked if we could take a long walk, like we had done so many times before. Knowing exactly what I was talking about, he was soon dressed and we were out in the night air. He said he was a bit surprised by my urgency and asked if everything was alright, or had I come up with new questions. I just stopped dead in my tracks and hugged him for a long time. We found a bench and sat down when he asked me what was wrong. I told him I was reliving a day, right then and there.

He was surprised but not shocked. He smiled and asked me what I had done with the day. I recounted the events with my family, all the fun I had with Kyle and Carrie. "Dad, in the future, my memories are so different from what we did last night. Every day events used to be something I hurried through because I was tired from the day, and I was just trying to get on to the next task in the night. My reward was the time I could sit quietly in my chair and relax before I went to bed... but last night, I calmed down and really focused on Kyle and Carrie, not the tasks at hand. When we made dinner, I really wanted to know what Carrie and Kyle had done that day. It didn't matter what we were doing, what mattered was

we were doing it together. When we had bath time, I enjoyed listening to Kyle make up stories and giggle as we played with his toy boats. His imagination is incredible. Washing his hair was the side event, not the main focus. When I read Kyle a book at bed time, I asked him how he interpreted the story, instead of just counting down the pages until I turned off the light. I'm ashamed to say this, but I know I often completely missed what Kyle would tell me because I wasn't paying attention. I was lost somewhere in my own thoughts. Dad, I was missing out on the important things... my focus was all wrong."

"Bobby, don't be too hard on yourself. Unfortunately, that's how most people are. Our focus is typically on what's next, and not on the present... whether that's the next event of the day, or the next season of the year, or of our lives for that matter. The old saying, 'stop and smell the roses' is actually very insightful. I think that's why grand-parents enjoy their grand-children so much. Maybe it's because they see their time as limited, but they make the most of their second chance at those daily events, and they take the time to enjoy the people involved. In many ways it is similar to the urgency we feel when we use a Banked Day. It seems everything always comes back to having the right perspective, doesn't it?"

Then it hit me. Dad was absolutely right. When Kristy was born in the future, and I became a G-Pa, I took my time to enjoy her. Tonight, I was able to bring my grandparent's perspective to myself and my own child. As time would reveal, this perspective spread to Carrie and eventually to Kyle and his daughter; and I imagine it won't stop with her, as the ripple effect will continue to cross

generations.

"I'm pretty sure our nightly routine will be different from here on, and I can see how I can relate this perspective to other areas of my life too. I'm really thankful I learned this lesson from my Banked Day. Thanks for bringing focus to it Dad..." Then my face grew serious and I it was time to tell him, "... but Dad, I have to tell you the real reason I came back to this day." After some hesitation, I just blurted it out, "You see, just before I cashed in my Banked Day, well, you died Dad."

Now he looked shocked. It was as if he had seen a ghost, and it was himself. When I saw his expression, my emotions overcame me. He had only been dead for a few days and here I was talking to him about his death. My mind had gotten used to the disjointed nature of time in our family, but this was something completely new to me. We sat there embraced in a firm hug for a few minutes, and then I realized he was consoling me; typical Dad. After he recovered from the initial shock, it didn't take him long to think the situation was intriguing.

"Whoa, that's not something you hear every day, is it son?" He said with a smirk and a muffled laugh. Quickly his mood changed and he added, "Whatever you do, don't tell me when I die, or of what. I know I'll die someday, but putting a date to it would make it seem like a death sentence. Just tell me this, how will I be remembered?"

It shouldn't have surprised me that Dad was mostly interested in what his friends would think of his life. "You see son, your legacy is how you stay immortal here on Earth. My faith will

take care of me in the after-life, but if and how I keep my presence on this Earth is all based on how I'm remembered. If there is anything I should know, something I'm doing that will negatively affect someone, please tell me now. I may still have time to fix it."

"No Dad. You just keep doing what you're doing now," I said as I gave him a tender hug.

I spent the next hour recalling all the stories of what everyone had said at his memorial service: how thoughtful he had been, and how much interest he always showed others by making them the center of his world. I think my father was happy and proud to be remembered that way. I assured him he had many more healthy and happy years ahead of him, and I could tell that eased his mind.

My father spent most of his adult life loving and providing for his family and friends. He put them before himself and never asked for anything in return, but now I had a gift for him. Perhaps the best one he would ever receive. "Dad, I need to tell you about something that happens in the future."

"Bobby, be careful. Knowing about the future can be very dangerous. Some things are best unknown until they happen."

"I know, but this is different. I wish today was closer to the future event, but it was the only day I had banked before it happens. So today is the only chance I have to keep you from suffering in the future. It's actually very similar to what G-Pa-Raymond did for his son, which kept him from suffering the guilt of Claude's death. What I tell you tonight may not mean that much to you now, but it will make a big difference to you in a few years, and well, for the

rest of your life."

"That sounds serious. Okay, let's have it then."

"Dad, after you died, Kyle and I took a walk. He was very upset with your death, as we all were. Somewhere in our conversation, I shared the story about Cindy and her death."

"Bobby, you told Kyle? Oh my..." Dad almost moaned as he looked to the ground, "...why did you tell him?"

"Dad, we had been talking about your integrity and the lessons you taught me. I skipped the details about why you were there that night, and I focused on your sense of loss and guilt when Cindy died. I don't know Dad, it just seemed to fit well in the conversation. Kyle and I were upset, and maybe I wasn't thinking straight."

"That's alright Bobby, I can't blame you for that. Not thinking straight while in an emotional situation is what made me use that day in the first place."

"Dad, after Kyle turns sixteen and learns about Timmah, the three of us go on walks to discuss our gift, just like you and I do now. On one of our walks, not knowing about Cindy at all, Kyle came up with a scenario where G-Pa-Joe could have banked that day once he saw the accident. Then he could relive the day and stop Cindy from being in the crash."

Dad had the same shock on his face as when he first heard that scenario in the future. Before he mentally started down that road again, I jumped in, "But Dad... wait... listen... Kyle told me he kept thinking about that scenario after our walk...then he realized there was a flaw in his theory."

"I don't know son, it seems feasible to me. My father could have banked that day and gone back to save Cindy."

"But that's just it Dad, by the time you and your father knew of the wreck, it was too late to bank the day and make any difference."

"Sorry son, I'm not following."

"Dad, when you return to a Banked Day, you go back to the moment and place you thought to bank it. Even if your father had gone straight to bank the day as soon as the wreck happened, by the time he returned to the day, the wreck would have already happened. There was no way to go back to that day before the crash occurred."

Dad slowly turned his head and looking at me said, "Well, that sounds right. We couldn't have saved Cindy by banking the day. That doesn't help Cindy, but at least I don't feel so foolish. Why didn't Kyle just tell us it wouldn't work?"

"Kyle had been proud of his theory and didn't want to admit it had a flaw... but then again he didn't know about your story, he thought it was just a what-if game. When we were talking after your death, he felt terrible his mistake brought you extra guilt for the rest of your life."

"Now my mistake is adding guilt to my grandson. That day's negative ripple effect just keeps on spreading wider and wider."

"It's okay Dad. It was Kyle's idea for me to be here today. He knew I had a day banked when he was young, so he suggested I come back and tell you now. When we have that walk in about fourteen years, and he comes up with his solution, you can tell him the flaw. While it may knock him down a peg by not stumping us,

you will be spared the extra guilt for the rest of your life. Kyle told me to tell you, that it may also do him good in the long run. He knows he can be cocky sometimes."

"That son of yours is pretty special, isn't he? He's going to add a few new rules to the wall... that I know. When you get back, please tell him thanks for me."

"I will Dad. I know that will mean a lot to him, and it will ease his burden as well. Of course, when the day comes when we actually take that walk with Kyle in the future, it will rewrite subsequent events. You won't feel the additional guilt, and neither will he. That means we probably won't even end up having the talk about Cindy."

"Hey, I'm alright with that."

"So if none of this happens in the new future, I suppose we won't end up spending my Banked Day talking about this... ah... sometimes all this makes my head spin. I tell you Dad, the ripple effects of changing events in time are so widespread. It makes you wonder how much we aren't aware of."

"It's hard to know what you don't know, but Bobby, you are undoubtedly right. The ripple effects of changing events in time are hard to predict... and in this case, we have changed an event in time that was caused by another event in the future, which had been created by what had been changed in the past. I'm very thankful you did this, but you do have to wonder what else may be affected."

We continued to talk on the bench until the sun came up. Eventually, we made our way back to my parents' house.

My mother was pacing in the kitchen when we returned,

worried where Dad had gone. It was so good to see my mother young again. When she saw me, she just shook her finger and said she should have known we would be on one of our walks. After she scolded my father for not leaving a note, Mom made us both breakfast and served her jam with the toast. She told me of her plans to try to sell her jellies and jams. Dad just winked at me, and I said I thought it was a terrific idea, and I wanted to be her first customer.

I made my way to the door and Dad helped me put on my coat. He noticed a large bump in my pocket and peeked inside to see a huge wad of cash. He went to his desk and wrote down the name and address of his stockbroker. When he walked up to me, he said he would trade the slip of paper for just one word. I whispered, "Microsoft."

When I returned to our house, Carrie was already up and worried about where I had gone. I made my excuse that Dad had called me about banking business and that seemed to appease her. I quickly redirected the conversation by saying I had most of the day off from work. She was surprised but quickly asked, "Well okay then, what do you want to do with today Mr. Greenfield?" An open invitation if ever I heard one.

"I think we should wake up Kyle and take a little road-trip. How about we go to a certain park and let Kyle play on the playground, while we reminisce about a certain significant event we shared there?"

"I love that idea, and I love you too."

Before we knew it, the three of us were in our car, singing to the radio. We spent the entire morning playing at the park. We

stopped at a Dairy Queen on the way home, and dined on their famous corn-dogs for lunch. We were all tired by the time we got home. Carrie and I put Kyle down for a nap, and then we sat down on our bed. We talked for a while, about our day and just general daily things. I cherished every minute. She never looked better.

"Honey, why don't we take a little nap ourselves? I'll get up in a bit and head to the bank for my late afternoon meeting, but I'll just let you sleep."

"Okay, that sounds good. Anything you want special for dinner?"

"It doesn't matter to me, as long as it's with you and Kyle."

She gave me a kiss on the cheek and drifted off to sleep. I watched her sleep for about thirty minutes until I departed without waking her. Not to the bank, but to the future.

#

When I returned, I was pleased to see Kyle and Kristy's relationship had improved. They had always been close, but now their bond seemed much stronger. It didn't take me long to realize my change in perspective on chores and fun had served as a role model for Kyle when he became a parent. He was still a professional when it came to banking, but he was a father first. He made every attempt to be at Kristy's events, large and small. I could see his marriage also seemed stronger, and so was mine.

Closer relationships proved to be helpful right away, as my return was only a few days after my father's burial. My sense of grief was so strong; it was overwhelming. It was so odd that Dad and I had discussed his death just the day before. In some ways that

helped, but in others it only made it harder to grasp he was really gone. We had taken our last walk together. I felt sorry for Kyle and Kristy as the once generation-rich Greenfield family had lost another member. I was the last G-Pa remaining and I knew those were huge shoes to fill.

Dad had died in the warmth of the summer, his favorite season. We laid him to rest in the O'Fallon cemetery among other Greenfields dating back to Levi's parents. His grave was marked with a simple marble headstone.

While Dad's father Frank, had died with no regrets, I knew my father had one. Cindy's death had stayed with him until the day he died. He was also tormented by his feelings of resentment that Claude had been saved by Raymond's letter. He was happy for Claude and his father, but it only highlighted how he was responsible for the one and only death associated with a Banked Day. At least he had been spared the additional guilt of thinking he or his father could have done something to save Cindy. However, this cloud followed him throughout all the seasons of his life.

He didn't like to talk about it much, but sometimes on our walks, Dad would reference a recurring nightmare. Sometimes in his dream, he would see Cindy's car approaching and he would swerve off the road, saving Cindy's life but killing his parents upon impact with a tree. Other times he would dream he could avoid the crash all together, only to see Cindy die the next day in another accident. Still, the outcome was always the same, someone died. On one walk, Dad told me that just once he wished he would dream it would be him that died. He said that would help bring him some

peace. Even with all the charitable work Dad had done in his lifetime, no number of good deeds would erase his guilt. Forgiveness of that magnitude can only come from above. I know his faith was strong, and I know he is in a place where he now is at peace. His secret is safe with me here.

Just as I had told him, he had a beautiful service with almost 1,000 people in attendance. Everyone loved my father and he deeply touched many people's lives. When my mother spoke at his memorial, I found it interesting she mentioned the two days he had banked and relived with us. She went on to talk about what happened after each of those days. How encouraging and wonderful they were, and how they never faded or lost their shine. At the after-burial gathering at my parents' house, many people told the same type of stories. All were a testament to a man who had unselfishly lived his life as though those around him were the main characters in his play, with his role being their support.

With everyone telling intimate stories about my father, it was difficult to keep the secrets Dad and I shared for so long, as they had been such an important part of our relationship. I had to scramble a bit when it came time to decide what to have engraved on Dad's headstone. With Kyle's support, my cover story seemed to satisfy my mother and our friends. I simply explained the unusual term was something we shared on our walks. As Levi had been awarded the title of Major out of respect by his troops, Kyle and I agreed Dad deserved this tribute for his role as a protector of time. Dad's headstone read:

Joe Greenfield
1946 – 2017
Loving Husband and Father
TIMMAH

#

An Intersecting Path:

"My family is alright I suppose, but seriously, no one ever leaves this tiny town. Not only that, but every generation ends up working in the family business. I can tell you right now, I'm not going that route. I don't know what exactly I'll end up doing, but it won't be banking, and it won't be in O'Fallon. I know my decision will really disappoint my father and grandfather, but I have to do what is right for me. All my life, they have been dropping little hints that something big is going to happen on my 16th birthday, but I'm dreading it. I'm just treading water until I can go off to college and escape. I love my family, but there is nothing here that will change my mind."

#

XV.   Indian Summer

It's almost nine o'clock, Kyle and Kristy should be here soon. Sitting on my park bench, I can see my dear old friends opening their shops, and there's Marlin opening the bank now. Marlin is Reba's son, who eventually followed in his mother's footsteps becoming our head teller. Marlin had a full and distinguished career in the military before coming home to O'Fallon and joining our bank family. He is only forty-two years old, young for a retiree, but then again he joined the service soon after high school. Since Marlin returned to O'Fallon, he and Kyle have become great friends, often enjoying trips to the lake with their families.

Over the years I've been lucky enough to see Kyle bank and cash in two of his days, and hear how they changed his life and those around him. He had been almost thirty years old and Kristy was just a baby, when he finally withdrew his first Banked Day from his senior year in high school. He confided to me how rejuvenating it was and how it made him appreciate his relationships even more.

Ah, there they are now. Kyle and Kristy came over and I gave them both a big hug. Kyle said, "I didn't know you would be

here today... I thought you were on a business trip."

I smiled and told them both, "Are you kidding? I wouldn't miss today for the world."

Kristy was standing there with a big grin on her face, waiting for me to say something. I gave Kristy a big hug and wished her, "Happy Birthday and many more returns of the day!" It's an old birthday greeting my mother used to tell me.

She smiled saying, "Thanks G-Pa. I suppose you know what else happens today, don't you?" When I hesitated, on purpose, she jumped in, "I get my drivers' license today G-Pa...if I pass my test that is... but I should... I've practiced enough... I can't wait until I can take the car out all by myself... ah, freedom." Kristy shuddered with delight at the thought.

I remembered that excitement, as if it were yesterday. I told Kristy, "Hey, you'll do great, don't worry about it... not even the parallel parking part. I've seen you do it a hundred times... you've got it down pat."

She admitted with a shrug that was the only part she was concerned about, but she felt she would be alright. My suggestion that she might want to wait until tomorrow to take the test and practice some more fell on deaf ears. I knew she was too anxious to wait, and I couldn't really blame her.

With a look of excitement and relief, Kyle asked me if I wanted to join them in the bank, "I have an important story to tell Kristy on her birthday."

Knowing Kyle would be confused, I threw him the curve ball anyway. "Actually son, I would like to talk with you privately first.

Do you mind if you delay your story with Kristy for a bit?"

Kyle was puzzled at what could be more important than telling his daughter the story of Timmah on her sixteenth birthday, but he could tell by my expression it was important. Letting out a sigh and glancing at his watch, he said, "Okay Dad. I guess it can wait a bit. Kristy, meet me back at the bank at, say, two o'clock, and I'll take you to the DMV to take your test."

Now it was Kristy letting out a huff, "Really, we have to wait until this afternoon?"

"Hey, I know it's a change in plans, but I need to talk with G-Pa. Why don't you go home and spend the morning with Mom. You know she would love to spend time with her birthday girl. I bet she may even take you out to lunch."

"Fine..." Kristy said with a dismissive shrug, "... but I'll be back exactly at two o'clock, please be ready. That means no meetings or quick chats with customers. Two o'clock sharp, alright?" Kristy knew how her father could get wrapped up in his work.

"I promise. Tell Mom hi for us."

Looking back over her shoulder she ignored her father, but yelled "I Love you G-Pa," music to my old ears.

Once Kristy was out of earshot, Kyle asked me what was so important it couldn't wait. The street was filling with the opening of shops, so I suggested we should go somewhere private for this conversation. "Let's go to the small room." Grabbing his elbow we made our way across the street to the bank and through the bank's lobby, saying hello to Marlin as we passed the tellers. I could tell

Kyle was disappointed that he was not with Kristy when we walked down the narrow hall to the small room at the end. I stepped forward, grabbed the key from the alcove and unlocked the door. I entered the room first with Kyle right behind me. Once inside, Kyle sat in the chair and stared at me, waiting for my explanation. His expression left the room so quiet I could hear my own heartbeat. Little did he know, his heart would soon be racing.

Leaning against the cold, hard wall, I started telling Kyle what I had been thinking about for over a year. "One way or another, the old clock is going to look different tomorrow. I'm living a Banked Day right now."

Kyle almost fell out of his chair. He asked, "Why did you Bank today when you could have just come with us when I told Kristy about Timmah? You didn't need to use a Banked Day."

I explained, "Kyle, it's you I really wanted to talk to. When I banked the day, I thought it would be the perfect time to come back and share with you the wisdom gained during the winter of my life. Then you could share it with Kristy, bit by bit, when she was ready... but later, I decided I really wanted to be here with you when you told Kristy the story. So I figured out how I could be in the room with you and Kristy, without anyone seeing me hunched over the table banking the day. I would just have to make sure I was the first into the room and the last to leave." Kyle knew the story of my father seeing himself in the room, so he already knew the theory, although he smiled now seeing it in practice. "Actually, that is exactly what I just did when we entered the room. I didn't want to be seen before I could break the news to you."

With a gulp, I gathered myself and dropped the bombshell: "Kyle, as the years passed, my plans for today changed... well, you see... in my future time... I am currently dying in the hospital."

Kyle's knees literally buckled under the table. "Dad, what happened? Are you alright?"

After I made sure he was fine, I continued, "Well, I feel great now, but in the future, I barely had the energy to sneak away from the hospital and get here to cash in my last day. When I get back tomorrow, I'll do my best to at least get to the lobby, but I doubt I'll make it back to the hospital. The important thing is I got here." Chuckling I added, "I bet the nurses are going crazy wondering where I am right now. I didn't bother to make up a cover story. At my age, you just don't worry about those things anymore."

I wasn't sure I should tell Kyle this, but I did anyway, "I think you should know, Kyle, your mother passed on last year." Seeing Kyle's shocked expression I added, "don't feel sad son, she had a wonderful and long life, and felt no pain at the end."

"Dad, first you tell me you are on your deathbed... and now you say Mom is already dead? I know we are all mortal... but this is hard to hear. Why would you come back just to tell me this?"

"Son, if that was all I had to tell you, then this whole trip would be cruel." I touched Kyle's hand and smiled, saying, "My mission for today, now, is to tell you the most important lesson I've learned from Timmah's gift." Kyle leaned forward as I went on. "Just like Timmah, my best gift was saved for last."

"During the last ten years or so, I was dreading the day I would live my last Banked Day; today. The thought of it all being

over was too much to take. I was afraid if I used my last day, all the excitement would be gone. It's been so much fun wondering what would happen if I did this or if I did that… but then I came to the ultimate realization, you can live each and every day as if it were a Banked Day. We are not limited to just three special days. If we were, Timmah's gift would be a curse rather than a blessing…. instead, every day should be lived as if you just came back from twenty years to relive it." After blurting that out, I took a breath. Kyle was taking this all well, so I continued.

"So about seven years ago, I started living that way. At first it was a bit tiring to tell you the truth, but then it became my way of life. Your mother soon caught on, and without knowing it, she was living each day as if it were a Banked Day. Soon our friends were living like that too, and believe it or not, so were you. Now the expanse of our gift has grown even larger. People who have never heard of Levi, Timmah, or the little statue, now have our gift."

I turned to look Kyle in the eye and told him not to limit his special days to just three. Placing my hand on the statue I continued, "You have a more powerful gift than the one from the little statue. As my father once told me, you have the tickets to a great day in your hand… all you have to do is use them." I reminded Kyle of the story I had told him many times, of the night I proposed to his mother. "That day had actually been a day my father had banked so he could spend time with my mother and me. When Dad asked me to give them privacy, I could have just gone to sleep at Jimmy's house, but instead I took your mother to the park and asked her to marry me. I'm not sure I realized it at the time, but I had decided to

live that moment in time like it was my Banked Day. I made a conscious decision to make the most of my evening, while I was living it in the natural flow of my life. Kyle, it's fine to enjoy Banked Days as you would a warm day during an "Indian Summer," but remember the seasons of your life are in their sequence for a reason. Enjoy each day in each season without regrets of the past or desires for the future."

It looked like I was getting my message through to Kyle so I just summed it up: "My best gift to you son is this advice, live every day like a Banked Day, and live it with a sense of urgency and interest. If you do, you will end up with a life full of interest, for you and those around you." Kyle sat there digesting what I had just told him. Over the next few minutes, he came to understand and was in full agreement.

As we sat there, I was reminded of all the walks we had taken over the years; all our great discussions. Since this would likely be the last conversation I would have with Kyle about our gift, I gave him another chance to show up the old man. "Kyle, I have one more what-if for you. Have you ever thought about banking a day in reverse? To be able to see what the future looks like and then come back to the present. You would have to be very careful, but imagine the good you could do with your insight of the future."

Kyle looked a bit confused and said, "Bank a day in reverse? I'm not following you Dad. You sure you're feeling alright?"

I tried this analogy, "Do you remember the old Don Henley song *Boys of Summer*? Ataris did a cover on it about twenty years ago." Kyle has always been a fan of Classic Rock, so he

remembered the song, the remake anyway. "Well, in the song, there's a line where he talks about how we should focus on looking forward and not back… in fact he is pretty emphatic that you should never do that. Does that sound familiar?" Kyle thought for a second and then nodded as he remembered. "Some people think that when Don Henley originally wrote the song, he was saying you can't relive your past, so don't waste your time and energy thinking about it… but I disagree. My experience has shown me looking back is the way to go. While you need to plan for the future, I always look back to help me understand and live the present better. So, if you could bank a day in reverse, it would be like 'looking back' to see the future."

Kyle agreed and quoted the old saying, "If you don't study the past, you are destined to repeat it… but if you knew the past-future, you could change the new-future…" Then he dismissed the notion by saying, "…but it doesn't really matter Dad, since Timmah's gift doesn't work that way." I could tell Kyle wasn't in the mood for discussing what-if scenarios, so I let it drop.

Everything had gone well up to this point, but now was the moment I had been anxiously awaiting and also dreading. "Kyle, I have a proposition to run by you. You probably will think I'm crazy, but please hear me out."

"Honestly Dad, I think your future condition may be affecting you a bit. Do you want to rest a bit?"

That didn't stop me, I had to get this out on the table. "I think we should tell a trusted friend about Timmah."

Kyle jumped to his feet, pointing to the rule on the wall,

where it specifically said doing so would end the power of the statue forever. "Dad, what are you saying... you want to throw away the gift we've been given? Do you know what people would pay for our gift? You can't put a value on what we have... Dad, you're just not thinking straight."

I asked Kyle to take his seat and I would explain. "Kyle in the future, we... you and I have proven you can live every day like a Banked Day. This isn't just a theory. We are not limited to only three special days... and the compounded interest is everyone around us can learn to live their whole lives that way too... they don't need Timmah's gift, and neither do we." Kyle had his head in his hands as he listened.

Taking a long, deep breath, I continued, "While living a Banked Day is fun, we have to consider the risks involved. When we use a Banked Day, we go back for just the one day, and even if we are careful we can cause great harm. Without being able to stay there to monitor the impact of our actions, we can't correct any negative effects before they spiral out of control. The past version of the person living the Banked Day doesn't know how the future is supposed to play out, so they have nothing to compare the new future to. Think back to what G-Pa-Raymond told us about the Banked Day that resulted in Claude's death. If G-Pa-Frank had been there to see the resulting effects of his fight with Claude, he may have been able to save him from making a bad decision... but as it were, he left at the end of his Banked Day and the aftermath led to Claude's death. While it's fun to go back to a previous season in our lives, banking a day doesn't let us stay there... when the day is over,

we return to our natural time and season. What happens in the past after that is out of our control."

Kyle quickly jumped on this saying, "but Dad, Claude was ultimately saved when Raymond delivered that letter on his Banked Day."

"We were all very lucky son. What if history had been rewritten where my grandfather had not married my grandmother? Then all the Greenfield generations after him would have been altered or even eliminated, and certainly Timmah's gift would have ended right then and there. Plus, we will never know if someone else took the bullet that had killed Claude. Another family's history may have been rewritten that day, if a soldier died who had otherwise returned home alive." I could tell Kyle was moved by this argument, so I continued, "The risks of altering events during a Banked Day are bad enough, but they are greatly compounded when we use a Banked Day to fix something that went wrong on another Banked Day."

I was on a roll, so I brought up a second event to prove my point. "Another example was when G-Pa-Raymond left his life in California to come back to O'Fallon... that changed what happened here in O-Fallon... but we don't know what changed back there in California. Changed history on top of changed history... ripples on top of ripples... I'm not smart enough to know how or when that would ever end... but it's safe to say that lives can be, and probably were altered in an instant... caused by ripples of change that spanned unknown, and possibly eliminated generations."

It was before Kyle's time, but I told him that banking days

reminded me of the sonic booms from when I was a boy. I explained how the ripple effect of sound waves was similar to when a rock is thrown into water. Both extend way past where the original action occurred, past where we can see the full effects it ends up having.

"When I was a kid, hearing the boom was new and fun, but it sometimes brought problems to those who experienced them, like damaged hearing and buildings. Eventually the Air Force realized this advanced technology had to be kept away from the general population, to avoid these risks. I now feel the same way about Banked Days."

I had been talking a long time, but I had so much to say. I've been thinking about this conversation for over a year, and had considered many ways to convey my position. However, I knew if I went overboard, Kyle would feel he was being preached to, and I truly needed his buy-in if we were going to take such a drastic step. So I summarized by trying one more analogy, "Kyle, nature has ways to reset our direction if we decide to vary from our predestined path. It's like the limbs of the oaks in the park. Those trees grow taller even though some branches grow sideways, and similar to that, we strike out in tangent directions too as we move forward along our path. While our free will takes us down many side paths, I feel we are all destined to end up where we are supposed to be. You see... the wind may sway the branches, but they always return to their original position... that is unless the wind is too strong and the branch breaks. Banked Days can introduce unnatural influences that work like those hard winds...which even the strongest tree can't

always overcome. The temporary fun of living a Banked Day is not worth the risks involved, and besides, the gains are available to us every day."

This was a lot for Kyle to absorb. All the walks with my father and me had always focused on the positives of banking a day. We never discussed what would ever bring us to consider ending Timmah's gift. We sat there for almost an hour, discussing the pros and cons of my proposition. Eventually, Kyle came to understand my position and somewhat reluctantly agreed to end the gift. He said, "Dad, I'll agree to do this, but I have to tell you, I think I'll always feel guilty that I denied Kristy, and her descendents, the thrill of banking a day."

"I understand what you are saying son, but just remember the greater gift you are giving them... a lifetime of days, as if they had been banked... plus, you are giving them the ability to spread the gift beyond our bloodline."

We sat there for a minute in silence, and I continued, "I always tried to use each of my Banked Days to enrich your mother's life, either on that day or after... but it bothered me that I couldn't tell her about Timmah. Eventually I was able to share Timmah's gift with her, and it became a gift to me to see your mother fully enjoying life, each and every day. Kyle, this is a way to share it with everyone. We should take what we've learned and use it to help us all change our core characters... just as Levi did, to live each day with interest."

Before we left the small room for the last time with the power of the statue still intact, we needed to decide who we would

tell to end the statue's power. We had to be careful. Telling the wrong person might end the gift, but it could also lead to scandal and embarrassment. Let's face it, this is not an easy story to swallow. Our family business relied on our community's trust in our judgment, our integrity, and our sanity. All of which could be questioned if this were to become public. Just as we had a responsibility when we used the gift, we have one now while we end it. After much consideration, we agreed we would tell Marlin. He had an open mind and could be trusted to keep our secret. We also decided we should both be present when Marlin was told, but he may take the news better if Kyle were the one to explain it to him. Since I was only here today from the future, we really had no choice but to tell Marlin today. Who knows, my old self may not agree with our decision to end our gift; we couldn't wait any longer.

 As we were leaving the room, Kyle asked me to walk out first. When I did, I appeared at the small table. I looked just as I did standing outside the door, since that was me banking the same day I'm currently reliving; but it reminded me of what I looked like in the future, lying across the table in my hospital gown. I was only a few hours from returning to that time, with my likely death soon to follow. Kyle went over and made me a bit more comfortable by straightening my neck and pulling up my jacket. He leaned over and gave me a kiss on the forehead. When he returned to the door, he hugged me and thanked me for all I had done for him in his life, up to today and after. As Kyle closed the door, my vision of me sitting there disappeared. I only hope when I return to the future, I will have the strength to get to the bank lobby before my body fails me.

We locked the room, maybe for the last time, and walked down the narrow hall, past Kyle's desk and back out into the lobby. Kyle walked over to Marlin and asked him to meet us in the conference room across the lobby from the old clock. I walked ahead and sat at the table in the conference room where I could see the clock, it read 3:59. Kyle and Marlin soon entered the room and shut the door. While Kyle asked Marlin to take a seat, I continued to look at the clock through the window next to the closed door.

Kyle did an excellent job bracing Marlin for our secret, and as expected, Marlin sincerely agreed to keep it to himself. Kyle gave a brief recap of Levi's experiences, and when he came to the point in the story where Timmah told Levi of the secret, something odd happened. I'm not sure Kyle could sense this while he spoke, but everything became perfectly still to me. There was no noise at all, as if a void or vacuum of sound had engulfed the room. I sensed it was the exact opposite of the deafening thunder that accompanied the power of the statue. I couldn't hear Kyle speaking, although I could see his lips move. I looked out the window to the clock and saw the hour hand slowly move back to the straight up position. Then, the minute hand followed the same motion. Finally, both hands moved to show 10:42; the actual time.

It was difficult to tell how much time actually passed, but in an instant I could hear Marlin's voice break the silence in mid-sentence. "... but Kyle, Mr. Greenfield, that's a lot to comprehend... I mean that is an incredible story... still... I respect both of you and know you would always tell me the truth."

Even though Marlin was being respectful, I could understand

he may have doubts about our story. First I assured him, "Marlin, this is just the first of many discussions we will have on this topic. Trust me... it takes quite some time to get your head around all of this."

"Thanks Mr. Greenfield. That's comforting to know... but to tell you the truth, I'm not sure why you and Kyle are telling me this. It sounds like this has been in your family for a long time. Why did you want to tell someone now? There are so many things you could do with that gift... you could change the world with it. I've only known about it for a few minutes, but I can already think of several ways you could have used Banked Days to help so many people. Please sir... tell me, what do you want me to do with this knowledge?"

Kyle put his hand on Marlin's shoulder and said, "Marlin, it's time we trusted someone else with this. There are great lessons we have learned from our use of the gift, and we are anxious to share them... by doing that, we can multiply the gift exponentially."

I was very glad to hear Kyle express his thoughts that way. Looking at Marlin, I could still sense he had some doubts, so I added, "Marlin, if I were you, I'd want some proof that all this was for real."

Marlin tried to maintain his respectfulness, but he involuntarily smiled and said, "Yes, that would help quite a bit, sir."

"Maybe this will help then. Let me tell you a few things that will happen in the next few days. If they come true, then you will know we are telling you the truth. First, Kristy is not going to pass her driver's test today, due to failing the parallel parking section.

Second, there will be a break in the water main outside the building tomorrow morning. Third, I suspect the old clock will keep the actual time from now on, and I don't think we will have unexplained loud thunder in O'Fallon anymore." All I could do was smile as both Kyle and Marlin looked at me oddly.

We had covered more than enough to make Marlin's head spin, so Kyle suggested we let this all sit for awhile. That sounded like a fine idea to me and I asked Kyle if he would join me for a walk. Leaving the conference room, we all looked at the old clock; it read 10:53. No one else in the bank had noticed the change yet since everyone was used to the old clock being "broken." Marlin went back to his teller window and helped the next person in line, although I suspect he found it difficult to concentrate. Kyle and I walked outside, crossed the street, and sat down on my favorite bench.

After sitting there for a while watching the clouds cast their shadows across the autumn-colored park, I broke the silence. "Son, don't feel any regret about what we just did, it was the right thing to do, and the positive impact will be tremendous. God knows I've taken many paths to get here today, but I think this is where I have always been destined to end up. Right here, right now, with you."

Kyle gave a weak smile and said, "I believe you Dad, but it will just take a little time for all this to settle in." I stayed quiet and let him work through his thoughts. "I've been planning this day for a long time, and this isn't how I thought today would go. Maybe you're right... try as I might with my free will... I was predestined to this day too." Another long pause and Kyle continued, "I guess

I'd better think of another story to tell Kristy when she comes back this afternoon." Then he asked me, "So anyway, how did you remember the broken water main would happen tomorrow?"

"Some events in life are just vividly entrenched in your memory, and that just happens to be one. I was walking up to the bank, like any other day, when suddenly the water main broke. It completely drenched me, along with Kristy's birthday present I was carrying at the time... something I will avoid tomorrow."

Then I told Kyle of the observation I had in the bank, "Kyle, when you were telling Marlin about Timmah, everything went silent to me."

"You know, I thought something happened where you couldn't hear me. I asked you a question and you just kept staring out the window."

"Sorry about that... yes, everything went completely quiet... but that wasn't really the strange thing. While it was silent, I watched the hands on the clock move back to showing regular time."

"Really... that's incredible... ah, I wish I would have seen it...that's a once in a lifetime event... well, maybe much longer than a lifetime."

"Yes, it was spellbinding. I saw the hour hand move straight up, and so did the minute hand, before they moved again to show the real time... but here's the thing... in the past, the minute hand didn't move back until the Banked Day was complete." As I sat there thinking it through, it struck me, "I think this means the day I'm living now... as a Banked Day... has just ended... and since I'm still here... I think today has become my present. If that's true, then I'm

not dying in a hospital bed... I am back here to live my future again." My heart was beating so fast I knew it would have killed me if I were still in the hospital, but I wasn't, I was here now.

With this thought soaring through my brain, I practically yelled, "I've done it! I've banked a day in reverse... I'm not going to die tomorrow." After just a momentary pause, I cautiously added, "Plus, I've seen the future, and I can use what I know to reshape it for the better."

Kyle sat there staring at me, trying to grasp the ramifications of what I just said. "Dad, that's incredible. How many years do you get to relive?"

"Well, I wasn't going to tell you the year I was coming back from because I didn't want you to count down to the day I would die... but this changes everything. I came back from 2043. That means I have twenty-one years that I get to live again!"

"Dad, the possibilities are endless on all the good you can do with your knowledge, but like we just talked about, we have to always keep in mind the dangers that can come from meddling with time. Then again, you now have the advantage of staying here to watch how things turn out. If you do slip up, we can take corrective action before things go too far."

It was nice to see we were on the same page and I told him, "I'm sure we will have many walks together to talk about all this. There's much we can do together with the knowledge I have of the next twenty-one years, and I am so glad I'll be doing it with you... this is going to be fun!"

After sifting through a few of the possibilities we now faced,

we took a moment to relax and enjoy a break in the clouds and the warmth it brought. Kyle looked up at the bare branches above us, "Dad, look at all those possible paths up there. Each one supporting another... that in turn, support others." I could tell Kyle was in deep thought, so I left him alone in the moment. After a while, Kyle said he was sorry to hear Kristy wouldn't pass her test today, "She will be very disappointed. I know she felt like she was ready, but I guess it's a lesson best learned the hard way. Kristy is just like most teenagers who think they know it all." I had to laugh and reminded him he had been the same way when he was her age. Then it was time for Kyle to share his wisdom, "I wish I knew now what I thought I knew then."

I laughed and patted him on the shoulder saying "Kyle, you should write a country-western song, and also include how youth is indeed wasted on the young."

Just then, a ball came rolling to my feet. I picked it up without hesitation, gave a wink to Kyle, and threw the ball back to the boy who was waiting for it, stinging his hand on impact. I said, "Not bad for an old man, but great for a really old man." Kyle looked at me and we shared another laugh. It was good to see him laugh when I knew he was still struggling with the loss of his last Banked Day, and not being able to share the gift with Kristy. Not in the way he thought he would anyway.

I grew anxious and told Kyle I had another person to see, and I just couldn't wait any longer. "I have a date with my beautiful wife. She doesn't know it yet, but we are going out to dinner, dancing, and then a night of romance. If you thought that throw was

good, you haven't seen anything yet!" Some lines are too good to limit to one generation.

Carrie and I now live in the big house on North Oak Street. It isn't far from the Bank, but I couldn't get there fast enough. So I pulled Kyle up off the bench and we started walking toward the street. A cool wind caused Kyle to pull his jacket closed, and he commented how he had enjoyed the "Indian Summer" while it lasted. I gave him a nudge as we walked and said "I'm about to enjoy the best 'Indian Summer' of my life, thanks to Timmah."

When we got to the curb, we stopped at a beautiful, brand-new, sparkling black Z Class, the new Super-Car of the Mercedes Benz fleet that I just picked up from the dealer this morning. When I opened the door, Kyle yelped, "Is that yours?" I understood his confusion as we had always been a Ford and Chevy family.

"Yes sir, it is. It's been my ride for the last twenty-one years. Well up to last year anyway, I had to stop driving when my health started to fail... but it sure is nice to see the old buggy shiny and new again." Pointing to the rear of the car, I added, "In a few years, your beautiful daughter will back into the rear bumper. Maybe we can avoid that this time... she was devastated when she dinged my car. This time I'll try to remember to park it in the garage the night she turns twenty-one."

"Dad, I know you are good with money, but how can you afford such an expensive car?" He added with a smirk, "After all, while we own the bank, we don't own the money in the bank."

Climbing in my new car with the ease I hadn't enjoyed in a long time, I closed the door and said, "Your grandfather made a

good investment many years ago and taught me a few tricks. I made my own investments which recently came to maturity. Hey, don't worry that I blew it all on the car. There's plenty left for Kristy's college education and more than enough to make us all very comfortable."

I could see the relief on Kyle's face that he would no longer have to worry about paying for Kristy's fast-approaching education. "Really... ah Dad... you don't know what that means to me. Kristy talks about colleges we can't afford... maybe now she can go to one of them."

I added, "I think she probably can. You should look for some other big changes in the next few weeks Kyle. I'm going to set up trusts for each of us, and I strongly suspect they will do very well." Kyle's wide grin practically split his lips at my insightful prediction. "Tomorrow, I'd like to talk with you about how we can use some of this money to ramp up our Helping Hands program. There are many who will benefit from our windfall."

My mood changed a bit when I thought about one possibility, "I'm pretty sure I'm back here to stay, but if I can't remember the future tomorrow, I'll need you to tell me what happened today, and to teach me how to live each day as a Banked Day... I know you can do it." Then I asked Kyle for a favor, "If I don't remember the future tomorrow, please don't tell me your mother dies before I do, or when my time will be up. That's one part of the future I wish I could forget."

But my joyful mood wouldn't let me stay focused on negative possibilities. Smiling again, I told Kyle, "Hey Buddy, just

in case, I left an envelope on your desk with a couple of good investment prospects inside." Kyle smiled again when he understood what I meant. "But all kidding aside, my real net-worth has come from the interest I've made with all my friends and family during my lifetime... and no matter what waits for me tomorrow, just remember that ultimately everything happens in God's time."

I put my hand on Kyle's hand, which was resting on my shiny door, gave it a squeeze and told him, "I love you son, but I need to get going... I have a date... I'll see you tomorrow morning."

With that, I pressed the start button and the car roared to life. Pulling away from the curb, I clicked on the radio and caught the middle of the classic version of *Boys of Summer*. My mind flashed back to standing on the stage in Jimmy's backyard. We were young, full of life, and had our whole lives ahead of us. As I sat in my new car, I felt the same way.

Today didn't turn out like any of the ways I had planned it in the future. This was much better than I could have dreamt. I wasn't on the verge of dying; I had years left to share with Carrie and the rest of our family. Just when I thought I had our gift figured out, it threw me yet another twist, and it probably will continue to do so for the next twenty-one years.

As if on cue, the line I had just explained to Kyle came over the Bose speakers. I punched the volume control and cranked it up. When Don warned me about looking back, I glanced in my driver's side-mirror and gave Kyle a wink. He heard the line, saw my eyes in the mirror, and bent over in laughter. I gave the powerful engine a

couple of revs and sped off towards North Oak, while Kyle finally noticed my personalized license plates: **TIMMAH**

Yes, my life has been full of Interest, indeed.

The End

Hardly!

The Greenfield Timeline

This story spans 200 years and seven generations. As you might expect, it became a bit complex keeping the story consistent with history and between the multiple characters moving back and forth in time. So, as I added to the plot, I had to develop a timeline to keep it all straight. My family found it interesting and helpful to see the book's events in chronological sequence, so I'm sharing it with you now. I hope it helps tie together any loose ends you may have.

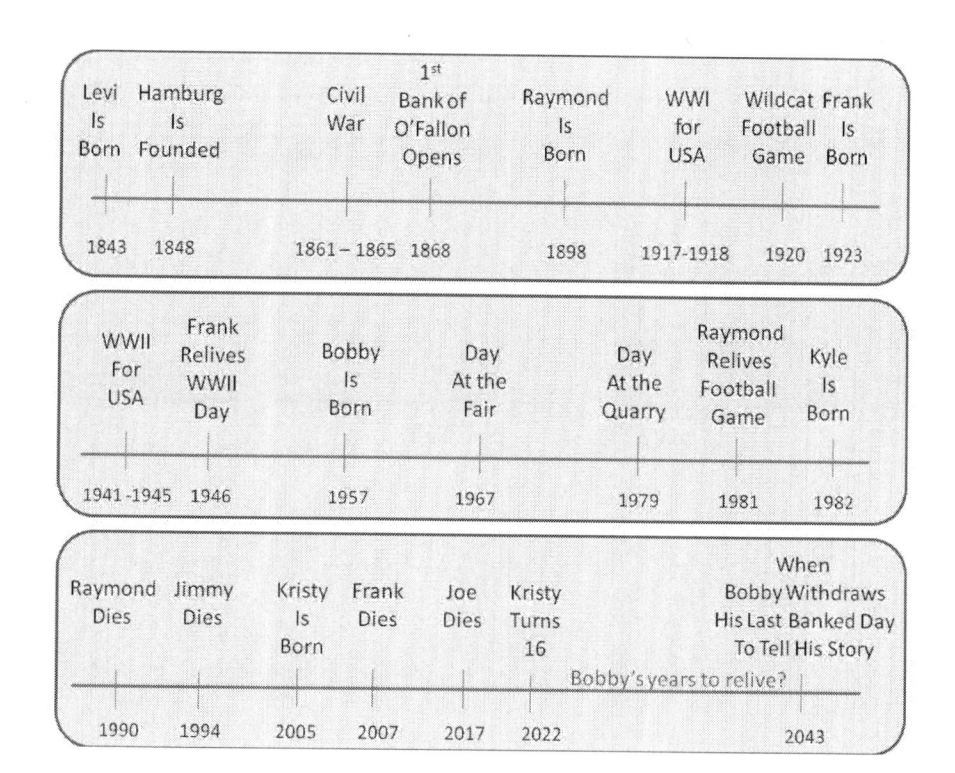

Note from the Author:

Thank you for reading Living With Interest: *Indian Summer.*

I hope you enjoyed the book, and that it will make a difference in how you live every day of your life – with *Interest.*

Look for the next book in the Living With Interest series: *Winter's Reprieve* - due out by early 2012.

You can check for updates, and post your comments and ideas at: **www.LivingWithInterest.com**

Best Wishes,

Robert Hammitt

Made in the USA
Charleston, SC
28 September 2011